HARD LINES & GOAL LINES

STEPHANIE JULIAN

Hocky Hotties!?

Steph

The odds are stacked against them...

As the backup goalie for the Philadelphia Colonials, Tim Stanton earned his nickname "Tank" by being an immovable force in net. Hockey has always come first in his life but, at thirty-one, he has an expiration date practically stamped on his ass. It's time to make hard decisions about his future. Retire on his terms or play until his body gives out? And if he stays in net, will he miss his shot to pursue the woman he loves?

As the daughter of an NHL Legend and the Colonials' GM, Gabby Mitchell has had to work twice as hard to prove herself as the team's public relations director. Dating a player could be career suicide, especially one on her own team. But no one have ever matched up to the quiet, broody hunk of a goalie who's her brother's best friend. When Gabby dumps her most recent mistake, a chance encounter with Tim leads to a stolen, steamy kiss...and a full-blown secret affair.

Gabby and Tim have skated around their feelings for years, but now their passion is reaching a boiling point. Will Tim's uncertain future and a scandal involving Gabby's brother tank their relationship before they have a chance to score their happily-ever-after?

Want to know more? Join Stephanie in her private Reader Salon on Facebook. And sign up to get all her news here.

Don't don't miss these other stories in the Fast Ice series:

Bylines & Blue Lines

Hard Lines & Goal Lines

Deadlines & Red Lines

ONE

"These kids are gonna be the death of me. I thought I was in good shape, but damn, I need to spend a few more hours at the gym every day if I'm going to keep up."

RJ Mitchell skated to a stop beside Tim Stanton, slapping his stick across Tim's pads before turning to lean against the boards next to him. The rest of the Philadelphia Colonials players were headed for the locker room, except for a few guys taking last-minute shots at the other end of the ice.

"Mik skates circles around me," RJ continued, "and I swear Marchenko laughs at me every time we do sprints. Okay, maybe he doesn't laugh, because I'm not sure the guy ever cracks a smile, but still."

Tim slid a glance at RJ before resuming his study of the twenty-one-year-old Russian goalie currently occupying the net at practice.

"You already spend five hours a day at the gym. And fuck you, golden boy. No one on the team can touch your points total. So what if two of the youngest players on the team are faster than you? Suck it up. I'm the one who needs to watch my back."

Tim nodded toward the player in goal. Kirill Alexeyev had a great glove hand, needed some work with the blocker, and had a tendency to drop his left shoulder. But damn, he was limber as fuck, weighed at least as much if not more than Tim, and stood a full two inches taller than him.

Tim had earned his nickname "Tank" years ago during his first year in training camp, but Kirill might actually be better suited for the title.

"Kid's getting good." Tim watched Kirill take another shot, this one going five-hole. "Needs work, but he's getting better every day."

RJ's attention narrowed as he watched Kirill take the next few shots. "Still young. Few more years in the ECHL and he'll be ready to move up."

Tim shook his head. "I'm not so sure about that. DeAngelo and Pilon are killing it in Reading. A couple teams have been sniffing around both of them, and Pilon's contract's up next season. He'll be gone. Another club'll offer him more money and an NHL contract. I figure Alexeyev'll be called up to Reading then. And with my contract up at the end of the season..."

He didn't need to finish that thought. RJ knew the situation. Shane Conrad, the Colonials' starting goalie, was one of the hottest goalies in the league. He'd had a few bad games this season, but Shane knew how to fight his way out of a potential slump. His nickname was Brick because, when he was in net, he was a goddamn brick wall.

But Conrad couldn't play every night.

"You're the best damn backup in the league." RJ tapped his stick against Tim's skate. "Still at the top of your game. No way they don't sign you for another season, at least."

Tim leaned against the boards, considering his response. RJ's praise was a nice pat on the back, but he and RJ had been friends for years. And Tim was a practical guy. He was thirty-one. And he was a goalie. He practically had an expiration date tattooed on his ass. And that date wasn't as far away as it had been a year ago.

He wanted to go out on top or, at least, go out while he was winning. He'd had a good year. Good enough to consider extending his contract if the Colonials were receptive.

Maybe.

Or...maybe he was ready to finally have a life beyond the ice. Maybe date a woman for longer than a couple weeks. Maybe, you know, have a girlfriend. Hell, maybe even settle down and get married.

The image of one woman in particular flashed through his mind and, not for the first time in recent days, he let himself consider what if.

What if he finally called it quits with hockey? What if he actually took a job selling insurance or cars? What if he finally asked her out? What if—

What if you just stop thinking about her and actually do something about her?

Yeah. Why didn't he?

Practice was over for the day and Tim wanted a hot shower, a meal, and ten hours of uninterrupted sleep. He could already be halfway home. But he'd been standing here for at least fifteen minutes, analyzing his replacement, and yeah, he had thoughts. And since RJ was his oldest friend...

Even though he wasn't sure he wanted to say the words out loud, he forced himself to put them out there, spoken low enough that only RJ could hear.

"I'm getting too old for this shit."

Without hesitation, RJ snorted. "Fuck that. You're having your best season ever."

No, he wasn't. He was having his third best season ever. Maybe. His goals against average was down from last year. Not by much, but it was enough to make him think this was the year. After this season, maybe he hung up his skates.

When he didn't respond, RJ leaned forward, getting in his field of vision. "Wait. Are you serious?"

RJ's question begged an answer he didn't have. The season wasn't even half over, and the Colonials were on track for a playoff run. He should be pumped.

And he was. When he was on the ice, it was still home. When he wasn't on the ice? He considered his options. Most involved starting over, leaving behind the career he'd spent most of his life working toward. Learning to do...something else. So yeah, he didn't have any answers.

It didn't help that he didn't have a life partner, someone to talk to about this. Someone who wasn't another hockey player. A girlfriend. A wife.

Shrugging, Tim shook his head. "Honestly, I don't know. I just know I'm having a lot of thoughts about the subject."

He watched Kirill drop his shoulder again as he lined up for a shot.

Tim liked the kid. Truly. He enjoyed the hell out of him. He was a goofball with an adolescent's sense of humor. Everybody loved him and if they didn't, they were an asshole. Two years ago, when Kirill had been drafted by the Colonials, he and the then-eighteen-year-old had spent a lot of time at training camp together. They'd worked together, trained together, spent hours talking and, despite their twelve-year age gap, had become friends. No, it'd gone deeper than that. They'd become as close as brothers, and Tim took the position of big brother seriously.

"Hey, man, we all get those thoughts," RJ said. "I just don't want you to throw away a career over a few points. This team is relatively young. They need a few veterans around to keep them in line."

Another shot, another dropped shoulder. Another puck

behind.

Kirill's head dropped forward, and Tim swore he could hear the kid sigh from across the ice. Tim straightened, but before he skated over to talk to Kirill, he heard RJ laugh.

Turning, Tim frowned. "What?"

RJ continued to shake his head, mouth curved in a grin. "You're a decent guy, Tank. Too decent for your own good."

That was a joke. "No. I'm really not."

Before he skated across the ice to show Kirill what he was doing wrong, he heard RJ mutter under his breath.

"Bullshit."

"NO, I'm not going to change my mind. This relationship isn't working for me, and I don't think it is for you, either. I don't think we should see each other again."

"Where is this coming from, Gabrielle? You're acting totally out of character."

"You're not hearing me, Rich. This isn't working. *We're* not working. It'll be better for both of us if we call it off now."

"I think you're having a bad day and are going to regret this in the morning. Did something happen? Is RJ's situation becoming more problematic? Why don't you let me—"

"This has nothing to do with RJ. It has nothing to do with anything other than us. *We're* not working. I'm sorry but—"

"It's obvious you're not at all sorry. But you will be if you decide to go through with this."

Standing outside Gabrielle Mitchell's office on the top floor of the Broad Street Arena, Tim's hand tightened on the doorknob, ready to turn it and yank it open.

He'd come to the third floor of the arena to talk to Gabrielle in private before he left for the day. He had a few questions about the upcoming fundraiser for his pet charity and, since she was the club's marketing and promotions department head, she was the person he needed to talk to.

Yeah, right.

Okay, maybe he'd had an ulterior motive. Or two. Maybe that conversation with RJ had given him thoughts.

Maybe you've been having those thoughts for a while.

Yeah. Maybe he had. Didn't mean he had to do anything about them.

He'd come up to talk to her, just wanted a few minutes of her time. But whoever the hell this douchebag was, he'd gotten here first. And as soon as Tim had heard the guy's voice, he'd known he wasn't going anywhere until this asshole left. He'd heard that tone before. Heard it used against a woman he loved. It raised his blood pressure and the hair on the back of his neck every time.

He'd been listening to this circular conversation for the past couple of minutes. Yes, he should've left when he'd realized this was a private conversation. No probably about it. He shouldn't still be standing here. But there'd been something about the guy's voice that set off Tim's asshole radar. He'd honed that radar during the first ten years of his life and now it was practically foolproof.

He'd learned to control his initial impulse to grab guys like this by the throat and toss them against a wall. But this one was testing his control. Gabby must've told him at least four times that they were through, that she didn't want to see him again. Every time, the guy had turned her argument around on her. He talked a good game, had a comeback for everything, and was probably used to getting whatever the hell he wanted in life. So far, Gabby hadn't wavered, and Tim hadn't been worried about this guy crossing a line.

Until now.

He gripped the doorknob, ready to barge in, when it turned in his palm.

Shit. He took a few steps backward but wasn't quick enough to make a clean getaway. At least he wasn't standing right outside the door when it opened.

Maybe Gabby would think it was a coincidence, that he'd been walking by her office at that exact second. Or maybe she wouldn't even notice him because she stood with her back to him while she stared into her office as she held open the door.

"We've said everything there is to say." Her voice held absolutely no give. Tim wanted to pump his fist in the air on her behalf. "I appreciate you taking the time out of your busy day to stop by, but we're finished."

Tim stilled, living up to his nickname. His teammates called him Tank for his style of play. He set up in front of the net and he did his damnedest to make sure nothing got by him. He wasn't flashy. He didn't move around a lot, and he wasn't as fast or nimble as some of the younger goalies in the league. But he was a fucking huge, immoveable object in goal. Pretty much the same off the ice, as well.

He wasn't going anywhere until this guy was gone.

After a few long seconds, Gabby finally moved slightly away from the door as a man emerged from her office. Expensive suit. Short, dark blond hair. Not even a hint of a whisker on his weak chin. And his mouth pressed into a thin line.

Tank didn't recognize him, and he was pretty sure the other man didn't see him because the asshole's head never turned. But Tim could tell from the way he walked like he had a stick shoved up his ass and the set of his shoulders...the guy was pissed.

Not upset.

He was pissed the fuck off.

The urge to grab the guy by the throat and make sure he got

out of the building burned like acid in Tim's gut. But he was quick to cap it off because as soon as the guy had crossed the threshold from Gabby's office into the hall, she glanced over her shoulder and caught sight of him.

For several seconds, she just stared.

Anger. Frustration. Hurt. Determination. All written so clearly on her face.

He totally understood that she'd be upset he'd witnessed her breakup. No one wanted an audience for something so personal and potentially painful, especially not Gabby. She was always so careful to keep her private life separate from her professional life. Something she had to work extra hard at now because her father had recently been hired as general manager of the club and both of her brothers played for the team.

For the past five years she'd worked for the Colonials, Gabby had walked that fine line every day. He admired the hell out of her for doing it and doing it well. But it meant she never dated anyone associated with her professional life. No coworkers. No sponsors.

Definitely no hockey players.

Which absolutely fucking sucked for him.

A familiar heat built in his gut, spreading like quicksilver through his blood. His cock wanted to harden, and he had to will away an erection that would've given him away. Given away this secret he'd kept for years. Didn't think anyone had any idea how much he wanted this woman. He'd never admitted his attraction, not to anyone.

But sometimes he wondered if she ever looked at him and considered what it'd be like. How they'd be together in bed. Because he sure as hell thought about it a lot.

"Did you need something, Tim?"

Everyone called him Tank. Coaches, players, media. Hell, his dad called him Tank half the time. No one except his mom, sister, and Gabby called him by his given name. And when she did... He got a hard-on. Every damn time. She didn't do it often, so that was a good thing. But he couldn't help wondering what it'd be like to have her say his name without a layer of frost coating it. That frost should've shriveled his balls now.

Gabby had a backbone of titanium and you rarely saw her sweat. She hated showing any kind of vulnerability with a burning passion. But now... She looked rattled. And that pissed him off.

"Yeah. You can tell me if I need to go have a talk with that asshole."

Of course, that was the absolute worst thing for him to say. He wanted to take the words back the second they left his mouth. Not that he didn't mean them. He'd meant every word.

But as Gabby's eyes narrowed down to slits of cool blue, her beautiful lips pressed into a flat line, he knew she didn't appreciate him sticking his nose in where she thought it didn't belong. That's where they differed in their opinions.

"I don't believe I need to tell you anything." That frost had morphed into a layer of ice. "What can I do for you, Mr. Stanton?"

Now, isn't that a loaded question?

For the past five years, since she'd started her position with the Colonials, he'd lusted after Gabby with a passion that burned steadily in his gut. A passion he'd never done anything about.

Of course, she'd never given him an opening. Probably would've shut him down at every turn. Hell, she'd shut him down even when he hadn't been thinking about asking her out.

Maybe it was time to rattle her cage. Now. Here. Tonight. Spill his guts and tell her exactly what she could do for him. Fuck the fact that she'd just gotten rid of one guy and probably didn't want to even consider going out with another.

But that guy hadn't been the right guy. And neither of them was getting any younger. He was thirty-one. He could see the writing on the wall. He hadn't been lying to RJ earlier. He had more aches and pains than he'd had last season. And who the hell knew what the next year would bring. He could be traded across the country or to a team in Canada. Or he could finally decide to throw in the towel and—

"Tim?" Her voice held a question, but the ice was still there. "Is something wrong?"

Fuck it. Crossing his arms over his chest, he rocked back on his heels slightly and raised his own brows. "I don't know, Gabby. Why don't you tell me why that guy acted like he owned you?"

She straightened like someone had yanked a string connected to the top of her head. When her eyes narrowed down to slits, she looked every inch her father's daughter. And since her father was general manager of the Colonials, the same team that paid him a decent amount of money to play in net for them, that probably wasn't a good thing for him.

Shit. He'd finally gotten a rise out of her, but it sure as hell wasn't the one he'd wanted. His damn mouth had gotten him in trouble again. When the hell would he learn? Probably never, considering this wasn't the first time he'd stuck his foot in his mouth. Probably wouldn't be the last, either. Especially where she was concerned.

"That's none of your business, Timothy Stanton, so if you're looking for an answer you might as well walk out the nearest door because you are going to be sorely disappointed."

Maybe she would've scared off another guy with the frosty bitch act. Hell, she probably scared off leagues of guys with that look. But not him. He'd known her for years, since they were teenagers and he and RJ had been in camp together. Then they'd started their careers with the Colonials within a year of each other. He'd been a second-round draft pick who'd finally been pulled up from the AHL just when he'd given up hope that he'd ever get that call. He'd worked his ass off to become one of the two top goalies for the club.

She'd been a newly hired PR lackey who happened to have a legendary hockey dad. She'd worked her mighty fine ass off for the past five years to get this fancy office and the title of Director of Marketing and Public Relations.

And because they'd worked together on his pet charity for the past three years, he knew she had a fiercely loving heart beneath that pristine white blouse with about a hundred buttons down the front. Buttons his fingers itched to undo. He also knew the straight, Colonials-blue skirt clung to a tight, curved ass he'd wanted to pet for years. The fact that he hadn't been given the chance made his gut ache with a longing he didn't think he'd ever get over.

Jaw set in a hard line, Tim slowly shook his head. She couldn't scare him away. Of course, she didn't know that. Gabby thought she had everyone on the team cowed. And for the most part, she did. Hell, even her brothers let her boss them around.

Not him. Of course, that didn't mean he didn't listen to every word she said. He did. He listened. He absorbed. He even agreed with most of what she had to say. Still didn't mean he was going to give up this time. That asshole had hurt her. Maybe she needed a reminder that there were other guys out there who would be more than happy to treat her the way she should be treated.

"That's not all I want. And you know it."

It was a gamble on his part, to blatantly put this thought out into the open. But after today's practice, he figured fuck it. What the hell did he have to lose?

Gabby's brows rose and her lips parted. He figured she was about to rip into him. He'd seen her do it to others but never him. He'd never really given her the chance. They'd always danced around each other, never taking a step across that line.

But now... She had to know what he'd meant. The question was, what was she going to do about it?

For a few seconds, he thought she might actually take him up on his mostly unspoken offer. She was a smart woman and he was about as subtle as a bull in a china shop. But after a few more seconds, while she continued to hold his gaze, he saw denial in the flicker of her eyelids and the way she sucked her bottom lip between her teeth. She probably didn't even know she was doing it.

But he saw and he knew what it meant because he'd been watching Gabby for years. And yeah, he knew how creepy that sounded. In reality, it was just pathetic.

"What I know," she looked straight into his eyes, "is that you shouldn't have been listening to a private conversation, and I need to head home."

Not the answer he'd expected. His eyes widened with an unspoken question, and she released a heavy sigh before turning back into her office and disappearing from view.

He should leave. She'd all but thrown him out of the building. But he didn't. Something about the droop of her shoulders and the way she shook her head as she turned away made him follow her into her office.

Fuck it.

"I'll wait until you're ready to leave. I don't want you to walk to your car alone."

Her shoulders stiffened. "I don't need a bodyguard."

He bit his tongue and counted to ten before answering. "I'm not saying you do. I'm just saying—"

"I know what you're saying, Tim." Her voice held a sharp edge that might've cut another man. "And I don't need you."

His gut clenched into a ball. That one hit a little too close to the bone. He bit back his first response, which would've pissed her off even more. Tried to find a more tactful way to say what he wanted to say. Then he thought, *Fuck it*, and opened his mouth.

"Are you ever going to acknowledge this thing between us?"

Fuck. *Fuck.* Christ, he truly was an asshole. She'd just broken off her last relationship minutes ago. And here he was, acting like a jealous prick.

Standing by her desk, shoving things into the large tote she brought with her every day, she looked over her shoulder and straight into his eyes, attitude dripping off her next words.

"What thing?"

He'd been expecting that exact response, but still, it made his jaw clench. "I guess that's my answer, huh?"

For a brief second, he thought he saw something flicker through her gaze. Maybe a little regret. Then again, maybe he was seeing things that weren't there. Because for the past five years, Gabby had never given any indication that she wanted more than this casual acquaintance.

Maybe it's finally time to give this shit up.

Throw in the towel and admit defeat. Except...he fucking hated admitting defeat. It's what made him a damn good backup goalie. He played better under pressure.

Still, if the woman didn't want him...

With a harsh sigh, he turned for the door. He was halfway into the hall when he heard her say, "Tim?"

He considered ignoring her, just continuing on his way. But it wasn't in him to do it. He stopped just inside her door, turned sideways so he could see her. He didn't say anything, but he made sure she could see him raise his brows at her. Her mouth did that flat-line thing again and damn if he didn't want to accept the challenge she'd just laid in front of him.

"Will you walk me to my car?"

TWO

Gabrielle Mitchell hated needing anyone for anything.

No, she didn't hate it. She *loathed* it. There was a huge difference in the meaning of those words. Hate, to her, included a component of fear. She wasn't *afraid* to need anyone. She simply didn't want to be in a position where she needed a man to save her.

Which sounded like she was protesting *way* too much, considering what she'd just asked Tim to do. The man stood in the door to her office looking huge and solid and—

"Sure. I can do that." Tim's voice, steady and sure, made her feel safe. "You ready to go?"

Yes, she was. Now that he was here.

Goddammit.

Nodding, she turned back to her desk to make sure she hadn't left anything behind. Of course, she hadn't, but it gave her a few-seconds' reprieve from Tim's dark gaze, silently asking questions she had no answers to.

Questions like, how could she have been so stupid as to get involved with that man? She wanted to stamp her feet and throw things. Mainly, she wanted to throw things at Rich's head.

Hard, heavy things that would probably barely dent the man's hard head. That bastard had made her doubt herself and now she wanted to run home, open some wine, and drink directly from the bottle while she alternately moped and raged.

While all of this ran through her head, Tim continued to stand in the doorway, arms crossed over his broad chest. Just looking at her in a way that absolutely did *not* make her want to sink her hands into his shaggy black curls and rub her lips against the dark scruff that covered his jaw.

Nope, not one bit.

Liar, liar, pants on fire.

Only it wasn't her pants that were on fire.

In a pair of track pants and a tight, long-sleeved white t-shirt that outlined each muscle of his chest in loving detail, this man made every one of her female hormones jump for joy. Even now, minutes after she'd broken up with a man she'd been dating for the past few weeks. The man she'd thought might possibly—

No, scratch that. At least don't lie to yourself.

She'd never, not even in passing, thought Rich might be the man of her dreams. How could she think that when the man who *actually* starred in most of her dreams was standing in front of her? Waiting to walk her to her car just because she'd asked, even after she'd nearly ripped his head off for caring about her.

It just wasn't fair.

"Gabby. You okay?"

Now that was a loaded question, wasn't it?

Physically, yes, she was fine. Rich hadn't hurt her. Hell, she hadn't missed any of the men she'd dated recently—and she was a little embarrassed to admit there'd been a string of them—after she'd dumped them.

"Yes. I'm fine."

Turning away from the only man who'd ever made her feel

less than fine, she slipped into her coat, gathered up her tote, and took a deep breath before she turned back to face Tim.

Why did you ever think dating Rich was a good idea?

Rich, with his perfect hair, flawless smile, and his connections to the wealthiest and oldest families in Philadelphia. Including, very distantly, one of the families who owned this team. He'd seemed like the perfect man when they'd been introduced seven months ago.

So maybe she hadn't been immediately sexually attracted to him. It wasn't like he was ugly. In fact, Rich consistently landed on eligible bachelor lists. Money, looks, family connections, and a personality that drew women like flies. He had it all.

Or so it had seemed. Recently, she'd noticed a change in the way he talked to her, in the words he used. Nothing overtly hostile or mean, just...off. Which was why she'd asked Tim to wait for her.

Even knowing it might've been a foolish thing to do. Because Tim wasn't a guy who let things get past him. Pucks. Slurs. Insults. Innuendo. If he thought something wasn't right, he let you know. If he thought you were in harm's way, he'd put himself in the line of fire in front of you.

If he thought some guy meant her harm... She had no doubt Tim would smash that guy into tomorrow.

Her jaw locked and she had to consciously loosen it so she wouldn't grind her back teeth into dust. Tension tightened every muscle in her body. She hated feeling like this. Hated feeling vulnerable.

But she couldn't shake the feeling she shouldn't leave the building alone. She didn't think Rich would hurt her. Not physically. But she'd never seen him as angry as he'd been before he left.

Maybe you don't really know Rich as well as you thought you did. You really know how to pick 'em, don't you?

"Gabby. Are you sure you're okay? Did he hurt you?"

Tim's voice made her heart kick against her ribs and her blood sizzle in her veins. Just as it did whenever she heard him speak. Or he walked into a room. Or she caught sight of him down the hall.

You're such an idiot.

Yep, an idiot who dated other men to distract her from the one man she wanted and couldn't have.

And why can't you have him?

She caught back a frustrated sigh and considered her response to Tim instead. She knew he wouldn't let this go.

You did ask him for his help.

But that didn't mean he was entitled to her every secret. Not that she had many.

She also knew she couldn't let Tim believe Rich had hurt her in any way. Rich had never laid a hand on her in anger. Hell, even when he did put his hands on her, there hadn't been much passion.

Maybe you should've heeded that warning sign.

Her chin tilted up. "No. He didn't. Honestly. I'd just... rather not walk to my car alone."

Those last few words had been tough to spit out, and he had to know it. Still, he made her wait another couple of long seconds. When she was positive he was going to turn and walk away, he gave her a look she recognized. Working for this hockey club, she'd learned early that you couldn't give these men an inch because they'd take a mile and leave a trail of destruction two miles wide in their path. She'd helped clean up enough of their messes to know exactly when they were about to make her life hell.

"Okay." He shrugged. "Sure. Let's go."

Her brows shot up before she got them under control. That was it? Really? He was going to let it go at that? Nope. She didn't believe it. Tim didn't give in. Tim *never* gave in. It was what made him a damn good backup goalie.

A smart comment popped onto the tip of her tongue, but she bit it back. He'd given her what she wanted without the third degree she'd wanted to avoid. So, she should just take the win and let him walk her to her car. They didn't have to say a word the entire way.

Except...she wanted to talk to Tim. She liked talking to him. Always had. From the moment they'd met. She wanted to bitch about Rich, wanted to get all the petty things that'd annoyed her about that man off her chest, and she wanted Tim to tell her she'd been right to dump his sorry ass.

It was foolish and irrational and absolutely wrong, but she wanted to talk to him, like they'd used to talk as teenagers. When he'd spend time at their house with RJ and he'd let her hang with them and hadn't talked down to her like some of RJ's other friends did, if they even acknowledged she was there.

Tim had never made her feel invisible because she was a girl hanging with her big brother's friends.

Stop wishing for things you can't have.

Practically biting her tongue, she gave him a curt nod then grabbed her coat and bag, stuffed with all the things she needed to do tonight. The season was in full swing and that meant her job became a twenty-four-hour-a-day profession.

She really didn't have time for a guy in her life, anyway, so it was a good thing she'd gotten rid of Rich.

And he wasn't that good in bed anyway so you won't be missing anything.

Today had been a clusterfuck from the moment she'd gotten out of bed and tripped over the bra she'd thrown on the floor, knocking her elbow on the wall and nearly punching a hole through the drywall.

All she wanted was to go home, veg on the couch and watch

Disney movies. Tonight called for *Tangled*. Or maybe *Enchanted*. And ice cream. It was definitely a Cherry Garcia night.

"So, you have any plans for tonight?"

Blinking, her eyes widened in surprise. And she answered truthfully, because she honestly couldn't think of any other damn thing to say.

"Yeah. Me, the TV, and a pint of ice cream. And, oh yeah, my cat, the only sentient being I want to talk to right now."

And wow, how ridiculously pathetic did that sound?

Ugh. She sincerely wished she could crawl into her bed and not emerge until she'd learned to live a normal human life with normal human interactions. She worked hard to present herself as a person who had it all together. For the most part, she thought she did pretty damn well fooling the rest of the world.

She handled the marketing and PR for a team of more than thirty male athletes. That meant, at any given moment, she could be dealing with thirty different fires ranging from dealing with the police after a couple of guys went on a bender after a bad game and ended up "rearranging" a private dining room at a local night club to shielding a player going through a really messy divorce from the press.

In the past week, she'd had to find a replacement for a sponsor who'd pulled out of a major giveaway at the last minute, made sure Hubert Straka's latest affair with the wife of a local businessman didn't make the national news, and navigated the continuing, tangled mess her oldest brother had left behind in California. All while handling the daily duties of a multimillion-dollar hockey club.

She was not the kind of person who curled into a ball on her couch in ratty pajamas and cried mascara down her face over another failed relationship.

Damn it.

"I didn't know you had a cat."

Tim's statement was so unexpected, she blinked at him for a full five seconds before shaking her head. Maybe that would help put her brain back into the right track. Then again, talking about her cat was infinitely more appealing than discussing the rest of her messed up life right now.

"Her name's Princess." She headed for the door of her office, careful not to brush against any part of Tim's anatomy. She wasn't sure her system could take the contact right now. "I found her in the parking garage of my building one night. She's missing part of an ear, her tail was broken and is now crooked at the end, and in the middle of the night, sometimes she cries and sounds like she's dying."

And she loved her more than she'd ever loved a pet in her life. Not that she'd had many. The turtle in grade school hadn't been very cuddly. And the family dogs had always gravitated toward her dad and brothers. But Princess loved her unconditionally. Unless, of course, she was late feeding her. Then she gave her the cold shoulder.

Since she was going to be late doing that tonight, she figured she'd be sitting on the couch alone.

Not waiting for Tim, because she knew he'd follow, she strode toward the elevator. About halfway down the hall, she realized she was practically running, but she didn't slow. Tim could keep up with her. Those long legs of his ate up the space between them, and before she knew it, he was walking by her side. So close, she could smell him.

And damn, he smelled good. He must've recently taken a shower, which made sense because the team had had a late practice. Reflexively, she looked at her watch and realized they would've ended practice more than an hour ago.

"Why are you still here anyway?"

Wincing at the sharp edge in her voice, she glanced over—

and up—at Tim. Another man might've been offended. Hell, Rich would've demanded to know what was wrong with her. He'd always wanted to know what was wrong with her. As if she'd done something she shouldn't.

Why the hell did you stay with him as long as you did?

Good question.

"I wanted to talk to you about the Sunnyspace event."

Relief flooded through her, which was ridiculous but, damn it, at least this was a subject they could discuss with no hidden agendas.

For as long as she'd known him, Tim had been involved with a local charity for homeless and battered women. She'd never asked, and he'd never volunteered why this particular subject was near and dear to his heart, even though she wanted to, badly. But it obviously was. Tim never made a big deal about his involvement. He preferred to keep his support private, or, at the very least, low-key. But he'd pressed the Colonials organization to contribute money and exposure since he'd arrived in Philly.

She admired the hell out of the work he did behind the scenes for Sunnyspace. Sure, lots of the guys had pet charities they gave money and exposure to. But Tim's commitment went above and beyond, for little to no recognition.

"What can I help you with?"

Those words came out of her mouth at least five times a day. A reflex. But, she realized, with Tim they weren't just words.

Danger, danger, danger.

She shook that thought out of her head and pressed the button for the elevator, suddenly realizing that she and Tim would be confined in a small box for the trip to the parking garage.

Her heart began to pound for no good reason. Okay, maybe she had a good reason. Maybe it was a damn good reason. And maybe she just needed to *not* think about what that reason was until they were out of the elevator.

The bell announced its arrival and the door opened. Tim waved her ahead of him. He still hadn't answered her question. And as she stepped into the elevator where they'd be confined for the trip to the garage, she realized she could see his reflection perfectly in the shiny walls.

Her breath caught as their gazes met and held. And held. And still he didn't say anything. The words to prompt him to say something, anything, were on the tip of her tongue, but she couldn't force herself to speak them.

He mesmerized her. It was the only word that fit how she felt standing next to him. Even though she wore three-inch heels, he towered over her. In bare feet, she stood a respectable five-foot six. Of course, in hockey, the men tended to be over six feet tall. And broad. Heavily muscled chests. Thick thighs. Washboard abs. And constantly black and blue.

Tim had a bruise on his temple, probably from the game Sunday night. She could barely see it because of his shaggy hair, but she knew it was there. He'd taken a shot off the mask that had made every person in the arena gasp as his head snapped back and his mask had fallen off.

He'd skated around to the back of the net, shaking his head as one of the refs skated over to talk to him. Seconds later, he'd skated back to the net, pulled on his helmet and his glove, glided forward a few feet, glided back, tapped each pipe of the net then got into his ready position.

That pretty much summed up the man his teammates called Tank. He could shake off a slapshot to the head and go on to save the game. And all he had to do was look at her the way he was right now, and she felt like she was the one who'd taken a puck to the head.

"So, I need a date to the gala."

She blinked, unsure she'd heard him correctly, even though she knew she had.

"I'm sorry. What?"

"I need a date for the Sunnyspace gala."

"Are you... I mean, I'm not sure what you're asking. Are you asking me to go with you?"

"Yeah. But it's not a date." He shrugged, making her feel stupid for being flustered. "I need someone to go with me and since you're going anyway, I figured we could go together."

Okay. This was obviously a "date" of convenience. Which was fine. Really.

Yeah, right.

But he wasn't finished.

"Think of it like a work thing you gotta do."

Is that how he was going to think about it? Like a "work thing"?

She studied his expression in the reflection, but it showed nothing. Just Tim, staring back at her with steady dark eyes, a warm chocolate brown that made her melt.

She'd never say it out loud, but she loved Tim's eyes. When he stared at her, like he was now, she found herself mesmerized. And that was *so* not a good thing. Especially not this minute.

Her chin tilted up, an unconscious gesture even she recognized as defensive. Quickly followed by a hint of a smile on Tim's mouth. Damn him. He had a beautiful mouth. Full and wide and—

She tore her traitorous gaze away from his lips.

No more of that.

It was on the tip of her tongue to respond with a smart-ass comment, something witty about his inability to get a date. But she knew that wasn't true. This man could date any woman he wanted. He just...didn't. He wasn't like some of the other guys who dated a different girl every night. Guys like

Straka and Pannebacker and Lindbach. To them, dating was a sport.

"Do you *want* me to go with you?"

"If I didn't want to go with you, I wouldn't have asked."

His tone hadn't changed, at all, but she swore there was a look in his eyes that hadn't been there before. A challenge. And because she was who she was, she couldn't ignore it.

"I guess we could make plans to attend together... What? Why are you smiling like that?"

He shook his head, shaggy curls falling across his eyes until he pushed them back with one big hand. "I'm not smiling like anything."

Her breath caught again as her brain came up with all sorts of things he could do with that hand. All the different ways he could touch her. How those scarred and rough fingers would feel against her skin, especially the sensitive skin on the inside of her thighs as he pushed them open—

Okay. Enough of that.

With a strength of will she hadn't known she possessed, she shoved those images out of her mind and focused on the here and now.

"Of course we can go together. I'll set up a limo and let you know what time it will pick you up. Black tie, right? Do you want me to—"

"I'm perfectly capable of renting my own tux."

Did she hear amusement in his voice? Or annoyance. Of course, it was. He was a grown man and perfectly capable of taking care of himself. He wasn't her brother or her dad. He was...just Tim.

"Of course. Then I guess that's set."

The elevator stopped and the door opened, a wave of cold air sweeping into the elevator cage, making her shiver. Three weeks before Christmas and Mother Nature had decided to bring winter on with a vengeance. The daytime temperature had barely hit forty. And yeah, she worked for a hockey team. Still, Gabby hated to be cold.

But she wasn't sure her shiver had everything to do with the air temperature. A couple of lights had blown down here, and there were more shadows than usual. On a good day, this underground garage gave her the creeps. Tonight...

Stop it. You're just freaking yourself out.

Rich was long gone. And she had no reason to fear him. She refused to believe she could have misjudged him so badly.

Shaking her head, she headed for her car, Tim at her side. She didn't tell him not to bother, that she could walk by herself the rest of the way. No, she let him walk her to her car, close enough that she could almost convince herself she could feel the heat coming off his body.

She had her keys in her hand, as she always did when she walked to her car, no matter where it was parked. She was a city girl. She knew better than to not be prepared for anything.

They reached her car in a matter of seconds, the silence between them stretching out uncomfortably. She didn't know whether she was relieved that she'd been overly dramatic about Rich...or upset that her time with Tim was over so soon.

You're an idiot.

Yes, she was. But she was also an idiot who'd said yes to a date with him. Even though neither of them had called it a date. Because it wasn't a date. It was an event they were attending separately but together.

Mental gymnastics much? Geez.

Stopping at the passenger's side, she clicked open the locks and was about to reach for the handle when Tim grabbed it from behind and opened it for her. Throwing her bags on the seat, she turned to give Tim a quick smile before walking to the driver's side. She expected him to stay where he was but, of course, he didn't. He followed her around the car and opened that door for her too.

Why did he have to be such a nice guy?

So not fair.

Maybe the question you need to be asking is why you dated a jerk like Rich.

A guy she'd been afraid would be lurking in the parking garage, waiting for her.

Sliding into the car, she gave Tim another quick smile.

"Thank you again. I appreciate you walking with me."

She expected him to close the door, to let her make her escape. He didn't.

"You want to grab some dinner?"

She looked up and their gazes collided and held. She wanted to say yes. She didn't want to go home to her dark condo alone, warm up leftovers for dinner or order something from the deli down the street.

She wanted to share a meal with a friend. Problem was, she didn't have many. And those she did have were married with children or in committed relationships. She'd learned she couldn't just call them up and ask them to meet her for a drink or a quick meal anymore. She'd learned if she didn't want to look pathetic eating alone at a restaurant, she needed to order her meals in.

Which was part of the reason she'd finally said yes to a date with Rich.

And look where that got you.

Tim didn't classify as a friend. So why was she considering saying yes to his questions?

When she didn't answer right away, he continued. "Think I'm gonna stop for some dinner at The Brig. You hungry?"

Honestly, she was starving, and she wanted to say yes. Wanted to go with him.

Wanted...him. And couldn't have him.

Swallowing, she shook her head. "Thanks, but I'm wiped. I'm gonna go home, take a shower, and crash."

"Aren't you gonna eat?"

Her stomach chose that moment to growl, causing Tim's lips to curve in a slight grin that was sexier than any smile Rich had ever forced out of his cold, thin lips.

"I'll have something delivered."

"Want me to pick up something for you? I can drop it off. You're on my way home."

Silence hung in the air between them as she considered all the reasons she should say no. And the one reason she wanted to say yes. Whether he realized it or not, he'd just offered to take care of her. Something she hadn't let anyone do in a long time.

With good reason. Don't forget why you asked him to walk you to your car.

But Tim wasn't Rich.

"Thank you, but I'm good."

Tim stared at her for another couple of seconds before he nodded, like it was no big deal. "Okay. Have a good night, Gabby. If you need anything..."

He let the rest of that sentence hang out there and she wanted so much to say, "Okay, sure, let's grab dinner," that she knew she had to get out of here now.

"Thanks for walking me to my car."

"No problem. Night."

Then he checked to make sure all her limbs were in the car before he closed her driver-side door, tapped on the hood of the car, and stepped away.

She forced herself to turn the key and put the car in gear and step on the gas.

And if she glanced in the rearview a few times just to see if he was still there, well, no one saw her do it.

"HEY, Tank. How's it going? You look like you had a crappy day."

Huffing out a laugh, Tim shook his head as he slid into a worn leather booth at The Brig. "Why, thanks, Sugar."

The bitty blonde waitress who always seemed to be working whenever he came in blushed as she handed him a menu he didn't really need because he knew it by heart.

"Sorry." She grimaced and looked over her shoulder, as if worried someone had heard her. "Didn't mean that to sound so bad. You just look tired. And that shiner looks painful."

"They always look worse before they look better. Doesn't hurt. You feeling any better today?"

Taking the menu, he looked it over for a second before deciding it was definitely a burger night. He'd worked up an appetite between practice and the workout he'd gotten in afterward, before he'd walked in on Gabby and the asshole she'd broken up with.

"Oh yeah. I'm fine." She waved away his concern with her order pad. "Must not have eaten enough yesterday. You want a glass of milk or a beer tonight?"

She never looked like she ate enough, but he wasn't her father so... "Start with milk." He'd save the beer for after he'd eaten. "And I'll have the burger tonight. Thanks, Shug."

"No problem." The kid flashed him a smile. "Be back in a sec."

Tim watched Sugar make her way through the muddle of mismatched dining tables toward the kitchen to deliver his order, saw her rub at her back with her hand, probably to ease the ache from standing on her feet twelve hours a day. This wasn't her only job. He knew she had at least one other waitressing gig at a place that made this diner look like a four-star restaurant.

"Tank, how's it go—Whoa, son! What happened to your *face*? Janine!" The navy vet who owned the place shouted over her shoulder to her wife. "Bring an ice pack for Tank's face!"

Grimacing, Tim shook his head at the woman who ran this place like a finely tuned machine.

"Jesus, I don't look that bad, Georgie."

"Well, you've certainly looked better." The sixty-something former Army intel officer grabbed his chin and turned his head to the side to check out his eye. "That had to hurt."

Shrugging, Tim let her examine his face, knowing she'd make an even bigger fuss if he put up a fight. From the moment he'd walked through the door four years ago, Georgie had practically adopted him. He'd been wary of her open acceptance at first, a hard lesson learned after Tim had signed his first professional contract. Everyone had wanted to be his friend then. But he'd quickly discovered Georgie didn't have a false bone in her body. What she did have was a huge heart beneath a gruff, no-nonsense exterior.

"I've had worse."

She huffed. "I'm sure you have. I'm pretty sure you weren't born with that nose."

She also had no filter. He snorted in amusement and ran a finger over the bump on the bridge of his nose.

"Nice of you to point that out."

Georgie's mouth twisted. "Hey, now, you know better than to get offended at anything I say. The nose gives your face character."

"Is that a nice way of saying it can't make my face any worse than it already is?"

Georgie laughed, loud and long,

"Damn it, Georgie, leave the boy alone. He looks like he's taken enough of a beating."

Janine appeared at the side of his table as if by magic. The yang to Georgie's yin, Janine had missed being a flower child by twenty years but lived her life by its mantra of peace, love, and understanding...and peasant skirts and t-shirts with her politics in full view. Today's choice: a rainbow flag flying over the White House.

"This from the Winnipeg game the other night?" Janine made a circle with her finger in front of his face. "You got your bell rung pretty hard on that slapshot from Devinski."

"Yeah. But I stopped the shot."

Janine handed him the ice pack she'd brought with her and he dutifully put it against his eye.

"Good thing, too, or you might've lost that game. And the team's doing good but not that good. You saved Brick's bacon that night."

"That's why they pay me."

"Mm hmm." Janine's gaze narrowed. "Something else wrong, kid?"

Biting back a sigh, he shook his head, making sure he maintained eye contact. Janine might look like a flighty hippie with her gray-streaked flyaway curls and hazy blue eyes, but she had an uncanny knack of knowing when one of her flock was distressed. Or, in Tim's case, frustrated.

"Just hungry. Long day."

Georgie took that as her cue to head back to the kitchen. "Ordered a burger, didn't you? I'm gonna add more vegetables to that plate before they send it out."

Georgie slid out of the booth, and Janine slid into the spot she'd just vacated, as seamless as if they'd practiced the move.

"No, that's not it." Janine's gaze narrowed on his. "Something happened. Wanna talk about it?"

He gained a short reprieve as Sugar returned with two glasses, milk and water, which he hadn't asked for but that she remembered he always got.

Growing up in a small town in western Michigan, close enough to the Canadian border that he could touch it, Tim understood the dynamics of a small community. Back home, it'd been a chain around his neck. Here, he had two, and they'd become his lifeline.

He had his hockey community, his teammates and their extended families. And he had this community, the one he'd found in a diner around the corner from his condo. Much smaller but just as important.

Georgie and Janine. Bernie, the old guy who parked his ass at the end of the counter every morning from eight to nine-thirty, reading his paper and bitching about the Eagles to anyone in hearing distance. Sun and Carlos, the young couple who lived in one of the apartments above the diner and who were getting married in two months. And Sugar, who'd showed up six months ago looking like a malnourished teenager with an ID that claimed she was twenty-two and that her name was legally Sugar.

Georgie had given Sugar a job and eventually gotten the girl to move into one of the other apartments above the diner, away from the rat-infested place she'd been renting in South Philly.

"Thanks, Shug."

The girl flashed him a quick smile then hustled off to take care of her other tables in the bustling restaurant. Even though it was Tuesday, almost all the gleaming retro-red booths were filled. A testament to Georgie's recipes and her assurance that if you left hungry, she'd feed you for free next time. He was pretty sure she'd never lost that bet. Not even to him.

"So?" Janine pressed, after he'd put down the empty water glass. "Do I have to drag it out of you?"

Suppressing a sigh, he shook his head. "Nothing to tell." When her brows rose, he held up one hand. "Honestly. Just a long day. Tapes this morning then practice for three hours and another couple hours in the gym after that. I'm beat."

"Hmph." Janine's gaze narrowed even more, and her head tilted to the side. Waiting.

And he broke.

Rolling his eyes, he sighed again, long and loud. "Okay, look. There might've been an incident on my way out the door but—"

"What kind of incident?"

"Just some guy hassling a friend."

Could he call Gabby a friend?

Can't call her anything else, can you?

"And this friend was female?"

He considered not answering but knew Janine wouldn't let it go. She'd sit across from him and stare at him until he gave in. Again.

"Yeah."

"Ah."

As if she knew exactly what he'd been going to say. And maybe she had. He swore she could read minds. Stifling yet another sigh, he stared at her in silence for several seconds before shaking his head.

"It's not like that."

"What's not like that?"

"My relationship with this woman."

Her head tilted to the side and Tim wanted to kick his own ass. Janine could read people even better than Georgie.

"So now there's a relationship."

"No. I mean, yeah. She's just someone I work with."

"So it's a work relationship."

His jaw set and it was all he could do to speak through clenched teeth. "Yes, it's a work relationship."

He had the sudden urge to bang his head against the countertop as her brows rose. "But that's not all you want it to be."

A reluctant grin curved his lips "Were you this adept at torture in your previous job?"

"I'm not sure I know what you're talking about."

The glint in her pale-green gaze made him want to close his eyes and bang his head against the table in front of him.

"Your talents were wasted as a high school counselor. Why the hell didn't anyone recruit you for the CIA? I'm pretty sure you would've made a damn fine interrogator."

Janine's brow rose and now she totally looked like the part. "Still not sure what you're talking about, but I'm pretty sure you're avoiding my question."

"I'm pretty sure you haven't asked me a question."

"Yes, I did. You just don't want to answer it."

He sighed, long and loud. "She's my best friend's sister. She also works for the team."

"Ah. Okay." Janine grinned. "Now I get the picture. See? That wasn't so hard now, was it?"

"If you consider the fact that I really don't want to talk about it, then yeah, it feels like I just went through hell."

"No. You haven't."

And because Georgie had been stationed in the Middle East for several tours during the past ten years and had come home to Janine with some hardcore PTSD, he wanted to take his words back immediately. Instead, he nodded in agreement then slumped back onto the padded back of the booth.

"It's complicated."

"Lots of things are complicated." Janine shook her head, her gaze never releasing his. "Tell me why you think this one is."

She almost had him. Another couple of seconds and he would've told her everything. But Sugar returned and saved his ass. As she laid out his meal, which included a salad he hadn't ordered, a double portion of steamed broccoli, and a slice of apple pie, she looked to Janine.

"Georgie said stop interrogating Tank and let him eat. She needs you in the kitchen."

Janine grinned and Tank tried not to let his intense relief show.

"If she knew what we were talking about, she never would've recalled me."

With a laugh, Janine slid out of the booth before reaching over to ruffle Tank's hair. The gesture was affectionate and one he'd come to expect from her. She took her role as surrogate mother around here seriously.

"Eat. We can talk later. If you want. You know where to find me."

Nodding, he grinned up at her. "I do. Thanks, Janine."

"Sure thing. Eat all your food. You're looking a little thin."

He and Sugar, still standing by his table, laughed at that as Janine walked away. When she was finally out of earshot, Sugar shook her head. "They're good people."

"Some of the best." When she didn't leave immediately, Tank studied the girl's expression a little harder. "You need something, Shug?"

Her cheeks flared with bright color, a sure sign she wanted to say something. "Actually..." She shook her head. "No. Of course not. Sorry, just caught me daydreaming."

As she hustled back to the kitchen, he watched her rub one hand on the back of her neck. When was that girl going to reach her breaking point? He'd seen women work like this before, two and three jobs just to pay the bills. Always looking over their shoulder, waiting for the past, or whatever it was they were running from, to catch up with them. He also knew from first-hand experience that sometimes women never got away in the first place. And that was even more infuriating.

Maybe he needed to be a little more—

"Hey, thought I'd find you here. You mind if I sit?"

Looking up, Tim's eyes widened in surprise at the guy towering over his table.

"RJ? Hey, man. What the hell? How'd you know where to find me?"

Sliding into the booth opposite him, RJ took off his ball cap and tossed it into the corner like he had a personal grudge against the thing.

"I asked Gabby." He shrugged, like it should be obvious. Like, of course Gabby would know where to find him. Gabby knew everything. "Didn't feel like eating alone again. I stopped by your place, but you weren't there, and your phone must be off."

Tim reached for his pocket and dragged out his phone. Sure enough, he hadn't turned the ringer on after practice. He wasn't one of those guys who had the damn thing surgically attached to his hand. Yeah, he checked it occasionally, but he hadn't since he'd gotten here.

RJ was one of the few people in his favorites list. Friends since they'd met as kids at a US Hockey developmental camp when they were twelve, they'd never played together professionally until RJ had signed with the Colonials before the season started.

And now that he had, they'd become even closer. Turmoil could do that to friends. RJ had brought a whole shitload of turmoil with him. Which was probably what'd put the dark circles under Gabby's eyes recently.

"Sorry. What's up?"

RJ's gaze dropped away for a split second. "Nothing. Just... too much shit in my head to spend the night alone in my apartment. Needed to get out for a while."

Yeah, Tim could definitely understand that. "Then I hope

you're hungry because this place has the best burgers in the city."

A spark of amusement lit RJ's gaze before it was pushed out by the strain that seemed to be his constant state of being these days. RJ needed to get some of this shit off his chest. Tim was open to hearing him out but...they were in public. And RJ wouldn't want to talk about his problems in public. Too many eyes and ears.

Tim was surprised RJ hadn't been recognized yet, between his movie-star looks and being a star player for a national league team. It wouldn't be long before someone figured out why he looked familiar. Most of the regulars here had gotten used to seeing Tank around. They knew he played for the Colonials, but he wasn't a star player.

RJ was a different story.

For one thing, the guy was chick bait. He drew female attention wherever he went. Whether it was the light brown hair that never looked shaggy or the blue-brown eyes or the way his face was slapped together or the way he smiled, RJ stood out in a crowd. The fact that he was a genuinely decent guy was just the cherry on top. It also meant when he showed the slightest hint of anything less than perfection, he got trounced.

Like what was happening now. He'd made a mistake, one Tim might've made himself if he'd been in the same situation. But if Tim had done it, it wouldn't be all over the NHL Network, ESPN, and the local news in two major cities. All for trying to do the right thing. And doing it the absolute wrong way.

"Hi there. What can I get you?"

Sugar appeared at the side of the booth, notepad in hand. She wasn't looking directly at RJ, but that blush was back on her cheeks. RJ did that to women all the time. Young, old, everyone in between. He didn't even have to smile or turn on the charm.

And they didn't have to know he was, although if they did, it would be worse.

Sugar probably knew who he was, but only because the diner TVs always played the Colonials' games.

"Oh, hey, I wasn't planning to... What the he— uh, heck. I'll take a burger and fries. And a root beer. Do you have root beer?"

"Yes, sir. Anything else?"

Tim gave Sugar a look, but she was studiously writing RJ's order on her pad, even though she didn't need the thing any other time.

"No, that's it." RJ flashed her a quick, heartthrob smile. "Thanks."

Avoiding all eye contract, Sugar nodded, mumbled, "Sure thing," then turned and headed back to the kitchen like her ass was on fire. Because that's the effect RJ had on most people of the female persuasion. Which generally made people of the male asshole persuasion want to punch him in the face.

"So," Tim said when it was clear RJ was going to make him work for every word tonight, "you wanna tell me what's going on?"

RJ didn't bother to deny or make excuses, just took a look around to make sure they weren't going to be overheard. The diner was busy, but Tim's regular table was in a back corner and the closest tables had just been cleared. And no one appeared to be looking at them with that wide-eyed "holy shit, look who it is" expression.

"Got a call earlier that made me wanna punch something, so I figured I'd better get out of the house before the damn reporters say I trashed my new place in a drunken rage."

Since RJ looked like he still wanted to punch something, Tim tried for levity. "Isn't your brother's new girlfriend one of those 'damn reporters'?" Tim grinned to let RJ know he was just poking at him.

RJ shrugged, not taking the bait. "Tara doesn't count. She's a sweetheart."

"I know that. Look, if you don't wanna talk about it—"

"It's not that." RJ shook his head, frustration clearly visible on his expression. "It's just... Christ, what a mess."

"Hey, man." Tim leaned onto the table, lowering his voice to be sure RJ had to listen to hear him. "You wanna tell me what the hell really happened out there? I mean, I get it if you don't want to. I've heard the rumors," and those were pretty fucking bad, "but I know you. And I know you wouldn't do what they're saying."

"Damn right, I wouldn't." RJ looked sick just to talk about it. "But most people don't know me like you do. They're willing to believe the worst, especially if a woman accuses you of assault. Jesus, I don't blame those women for coming out with their story. Clairmont had it coming. But I didn't do the shit they're accusing him of. The problem is some shady fucking lawyers are telling them to go for the big payday so they're going after me, too. Even though I wasn't there and can prove it."

"So what exactly went down?"

RJ kept shaking his head. "A few of the younger guys had a party. I was there for a few minutes. The doorman and the security cameras make it clear when I arrived and when I left. And everything happened after I left. Clairmont and Aube started a fight over one of the women. Typical asshole behavior from Clairmont. The guy's a dick."

Yeah, he was. Doug Clairmont had a reputation as a hard partier ready to toss down his gloves at the slightest provocation. He also had a rep with the ladies. Love 'em and leave 'em, typically in the same two-hour span. Asshole manwhore.

"So you left before the fight?"

"Yeah. I keep thinking maybe if I'd stayed, I could've broken it up. Avoided all this shit." RJ shook his head, his gaze practically stabbing the table between them. "I was on my way out and ran into one of the women. Literally. She was drunk and weaving all the hell over the place. You know me. I don't go there. Ever."

True. When people called RJ a boy scout, they weren't kidding. The guy never drank to excess, rarely swore, and always had a smile.

That smile had disappeared in the past few weeks. They were only two months into the season, but RJ looked like he'd spent the past six months being ground into the boards. Not physically, but mentally. Dark circles under his eyes, perpetual frown, tight jaw, as if he was constantly clenching his teeth. And you got the sense he was holding himself in check all the time.

The only time the guy looked like his normal self was when he was on the ice. He still played like the fucking amazing player he was.

"So how the hell did you get dragged into whatever the fuck happened?"

RJ shook his head, his jaw tightening until the muscles stood out in stark relief.

"I offered to take her home. She got as far as the door and decided she didn't want to leave. I seriously considered throwing her over my shoulder and just putting her in my car, but she was over eighteen, you know? I figured I'd get in trouble if I just shoved her in my car and drove away." He grunted. "Of course, now it's so much worse."

"I know they charged Clairmont already, but are they gonna charge you with something or just let the rumors keep swirling?"

"No fu—" He shook his head and his mouth twisted in a grimace. "I don't have a clue."

RJ looked up then, his gaze focusing over Tim's shoulder.

And his smile returned, the fake one that fooled most other people.

"Watch out. Plate's hot."

Sugar had returned with RJ's food.

"Thanks." RJ nodded. "This looks great."

Sugar's smile reappeared for a split second. "Let me know if you need anything else."

Then she disappeared back to the kitchen before Tim had a chance to ask for a refill for his water. RJ either didn't notice Sugar's tongue-tied interest or he took it in stride. Tim just shook his head. RJ didn't notice that, either. Couldn't blame the guy. He had a lot of heavy shit on his mind.

RJ fell silent again, until Tim prodded him. "So what're you gonna do?"

RJ sighed. "I honestly don't have a clue right now. We're talking to lawyers but... You know what?" Shaking his head, RJ looked him in the eyes. "I don't want to talk about it anymore. Enough about me. Why don't you tell me what you did to my sister? Gabby seemed pissed off at you. What happened? You two don't typically get on each other's nerves."

RJ's shit-eating grin made Tim grit his teeth, though he was careful not to let his expression give him away. "Why do you think I did something?"

"Because, besides Brody and me, you're the only one who gets under her skin."

Hmm. "Bullshit. Lot of the guys piss her off."

"True. But she was in a weird mood tonight."

It was on the tip of Tim's tongue to tell RJ about the guy in Gabby's office, but that would be too much like ratting her out. Besides, she'd handled it. And if Tim ever saw the guy hanging around again, he'd punt his ass down Broad Street.

"Yeah, well, don't blame me for that. We were talking about the fundraiser for the shelter."

"Oh, yeah, forgot that was coming up. I'll be making my donation anonymously this year. Don't want anyone to read anything into it. Just want to donate." RJ paused. "You still trying to get your mom and sister to move here?"

Tim knew RJ wasn't deliberately pushing his buttons, but a familiar ache in the pit of his stomach threatened to drag his mood down farther. When that happened, that black mood could ride him for days. And he didn't have the luxury of wallowing in that pit now. Not with the team doing well and him playing more games to give Shane a rest going into the back half of the season.

RJ was one of the few people Tim trusted and had told him the backstory years ago, one night at some hockey camp. He couldn't even remember which one; it seemed like forever ago.

"No. I'm planning to go home for a couple days for the holiday break, but—" Tim sighed, shaking his head. "I have to talk to my sister first. Don't want to stir shit up. If my dad's gonna be home most of the time..."

He had to force out that last sentence. If he were honest, he'd love to stir shit up with his dad. But he knew it'd upset his mom and sister, and he wanted to avoid that at all costs. He didn't want to put them in the middle of an already impossible situation.

"Situation sucks all around."

Tim nodded at RJ's soft comment. RJ knew more than anyone but Tim's family about the issues between Tim and his dad. But even RJ didn't know everything. Probably never would. Unless Tim's asshole dad showed up and opened his damn mouth. The last time Tim had talked to his mom, she'd mentioned his dad had threatened to come to a game again. Of course, his mom didn't present it like that.

But if his dad did show up... Tim would either have to avoid him or put his fist in his dad's face. Because if his dad started talking shit…

He'd been after his mom and sister to pack up and move the hell away from that fucking small town where the neighbors knew everyone's business but still managed not to see what was going on right in front of their face. Or they saw it but looked away and pretended not to.

"Tank? You okay?"

Mentally shaking off those thought, he nodded. "I'm fine. I should be asking you that question."

RJ just shook his head. "I don't think things are gonna be okay for a while."

Tim hoped like hell RJ was wrong. If he wasn't, Tim was worried RJ might never overcome this shit. He was about to say that out loud when Georgie walked up to his table, a grin on her face.

Tim's gaze narrowed.

"Hey, Tank, I got a favor to ask."

THREE

Gabby opened the door to her apartment, juggling her purse, her tote, and the bag the doorman had given her.

He'd offered to bring it up for her, but she'd waved him off with a smile. And regretted it five feet from the desk. The damn thing was heavy, filled with cat food. She heaved a sigh of relief the second she dropped everything on her dining room table seconds after she opened the front door.

With a little groan, she kicked off her shoes and headed for the fridge. She *so* deserved the Flying Monkeys Chocolate Manifesto she had waiting. Downing a quarter of the bottle on her first sip, she came up for air for a second to head back to the living room, where she sank onto the couch. Seconds later, her lap was filled with twenty pounds of warm, purring, coal-black fur.

"Hey there, Princess. And how did you spend your day?"

The huge cat meowed at her, butting her head against Gabby's chin and somehow managing to find a way to dig her claws into the places where it would hurt the most. Gabby grimaced but didn't move, knowing if she did, Princess would jump down and glare at her from the floor, highly offended that Gabby had dared to pet her.

The former stray who Gabby had found cowering in a corner of her apartment's underground garage one night about a year ago, her ear gnawed and her paw bleeding, had moved into Gabby's house after she'd spent a small fortune to have the furball fixed up.

Of course, the damn cat thought she owned the place now, but that was okay. Gabby enjoyed the company.

"Bet you had a great day. Laid in the sun for hours. Not a care in the world. Probably didn't even miss me, did you?"

As if she'd said something ridiculous, Princess gave her another haughty look before turning tail and jumping off her lap. She trotted off toward the kitchen then sat and looked over her shoulder at Gabby. Her gaze clearly demanded she be fed and now.

With an amused huff, Gabby pushed off the couch and served up supper for her furry overlord.

Leaning back against the counter, watching Princess scarf her dinner, she shook her head and took another sip of her beer. At the rate she was drinking, she'd be buzzed before she got any food in her and then she'd just sit down and inhale junk the rest of the night.

Which definitely wouldn't be good for her dedication to being healthier this year.

"I'm sure you'll be happy to know I got rid of Rich. You always thought he was a douchebag, didn't you?"

Princess ignored her, happy to have been fed so she could now ignore the emotionally needy human who controlled the food. Gabby didn't blame Princess. She wouldn't want to listen to her whine, either.

Should've taken Tim up on his offer for dinner.

In the security and quiet of her apartment, she could allow herself to answer that truthfully.

"Wish I could have."

Of all the things she wished she could do, Tim Stanton sat at the top of the list.

Shaking that thought out of her head before it could take hold, she sucked down the rest of her beer then headed to her bedroom for a shower. Dropping her clothes on the floor by her bed, she set the water temperature just shy of scalding then stepped under the spray and let it wash away the day. Wash away the stress left behind by her breakup with Rich. But it was going to take more than a twenty-minute shower to do that.

Back in her kitchen in tights, a cami, a slouchy fleece top that covered her ass, and thick socks, she opened the fridge, knowing she was about to be disappointed by the lack of anything resembling a decent meal.

Turning, she found Princess sitting on the counter, where she wasn't supposed to be, watching her with haughty disdain.

"Don't look at me like that. You got your dinner. I need to find mine. Guess it's a phone call tonight."

Tim's mention earlier and RJ's call looking for Tim had embedded it in her head and now the only thing she wanted right now was a meatloaf dinner from The Brig.

Well, not the only thing.

But since the only thing she could order over the phone was dinner, that's what she did.

Flipping on the NHL Network while she waited, she braced for any mention of RJ, breathing easier only when the hosts signed off for the night. Getting up when she needed another beer, she glanced at the table where she'd set her tote with her laptop. She really should take a look at the social media postings for the rest of the week, make sure everything was ready to go.

She had only just opened her laptop when the doorman rang.

"You have a food delivery, Miss Mitchell. May I send him up?"

"Yes, thank you, Mr. Jamieson."

"Of course. You have a good night, Miss Mitchell."

Rifling through her purse for her wallet, she got out a tip for Shane, The Brig's delivery guy, then headed for the door. The knock came seconds later.

"Hey, Sha—" Her mouth dropped open. "What the hell are you doing here?"

She wanted to take back her words immediately, but the man standing outside her door was definitely not Shane. No, Tim stood there, a half-assed grin on his lips and holding a bag she assumed held her food.

"Tell me how you're really feeling, Gabs." He held up the bag and shook it. "I believe you ordered dinner. Georgie asked me to deliver, since Shane was out and you're on my way home."

Still slightly stunned to see Tim standing at her door, Gabby shook her head.

"Excuse me?"

Tim's grin widened. "Not that hard to figure out. Georgie knows we're friends. Or whatever." One broad shoulder lifted. "And I practically live around the corner. Besides, I don't usually tell Georgie no. I'm pretty sure she could take me."

As her shock at seeing Tim at her door began to fade, Gabby realized she wasn't unhappy to see him. Far from it, if she was honest. Her heart rate began to race, and she had to swallow hard because *Tim* was standing just outside her door, so close to being inside her apartment that all she had to do was reach for his hand and tug him inside.

What she'd do with him then was something she couldn't allow herself to think about, because if she did...

"Gabby? You want your food? You don't have tip me, you know."

His flip comment about the tip finally nudged her out of her head. "Of course. Sorry. Thanks." She took the bag from his hand but didn't move to close the door. She didn't want to shut him out and she didn't want to eat alone tonight. It was just too quiet in her apartment, even with the TV on.

Before he could leave, she blurted out, "Do you want to come in?"

She caught his surprise in the lift of his eyebrows a second before he brought it back into line and nodded.

"Sure." He held up his other hand and the bag she hadn't noticed before. "I've got dessert, if you're interested. I'll share."

Swallowing hard, she nearly choked on her tongue. Was he offering himself up on a platter, covered in hot fudge and whipped cream? Because if he was, she'd definitely be okay with that. The fact that she'd never thought about Rich naked and covered in sticky, sugary treats should've been a huge, flashing red warning sign.

Since it wasn't, she nodded and waved him inside. The second he crossed the threshold, she gave herself permission to ignore the little voice in her head that kept saying this was a bad idea. That she'd made a huge mistake.

Because even if she had, at this very moment, she didn't give a damn. She wanted to talk to someone. Anyone.

Bullshit. You want to talk to Tim.

Fine. So what if she did?

Closing the door behind him, she flashed a little smile then nodded toward the living area.

"I was just finishing some work."

"Do you work through every meal?"

The look he gave her made her stomach twist into a little knot. He looked concerned, like he actually cared that she spent way too much time working. Rich had taken her long hours in stride, for the most part. Unless they'd impacted him in some way. Then he made sure she knew just how much of an inconvenience they were. Rich really was a dick.

Too bad you're just figuring that out now.

"Not every meal, no." Just most of them. "Sometimes, I actually get a lot more work done here than I do at the office. Too many interruptions there."

Setting the food on the table in front of the couch, she motioned for him to take a seat then headed for the kitchen for plates and utensils.

"You want something to dri—Oh!"

She'd turned to call over her shoulder only to find Tim had followed her and now stood only inches away. Making her open-concept kitchen seem really, really tight at the moment. And making it hard for her to breathe normally.

"Sure. Water's fine unless you've got beer. I could go for a beer."

"Guess it's your lucky night."

Even before the words left her lips, she wanted to take them back. She totally sounded like she was flirting with him. Did he think she was flirting with him? She met his gaze and found him smiling at her. Ruefully. As if he knew exactly what she was thinking and was totally amused by her.

Lifting her eyebrows, she silently dared him to say something. This man was smarter than she usually gave men credit for being. But this was Tim. Tim wasn't just any other man. At least not to her.

"I'll take whatever you've got."

She had to bite her tongue against the urge to *actually* flirt with him. To be the kind of woman who grinned up at him and told him she'd give him whatever he wanted.

Biting back a sigh, she turned to the fridge. "You want dark or light?"

"What are my choices?"

Behind her, she felt him move closer, sending her blood racing through her veins.

"Damn. Didn't realize you were a beer connoisseur." His breath brushed against her neck, raising gooseflesh. Damn him. "How many kinds do you have in there?"

"A few. I prefer chocolate porters, but I've got a couple different IPAs for my brothers if you're not into dark beer."

"I'll split a porter with you. Your choice."

She didn't question him. A lot of the guys barely touched alcohol during the season. She hadn't known Tim was one of them. Then again, she didn't know all there was to know about him.

And you're not going to, either.

She told her inner bitch to shut the fuck up and got a bottle out of the fridge. After she poured them each a glass, she led him back to the living room and sat on the couch, expecting him to take the chair across. Instead, he sat at the other end of the couch.

Close enough for her to touch. And she wanted to touch him. Which she couldn't do. Wouldn't do. No matter how much she wanted to.

"You gonna eat?" He pointed to the bag she'd put on the table in front of the couch. "Don't let it get cold. Especially if you've got Georgie's meatloaf in there. She makes the best damn meatloaf I've ever tasted."

"Better than your own mother's?"

She'd meant it as a tease, a nothing little comment to lighten the mood. But something crossed his expression, too quick for her to figure out what it was before it was gone. Something to do with his mom? He didn't talk much about his family, but she knew he had a good relationship with his mom and sister. She also knew he had a not-so-good relationship with his dad. She wanted him to talk to her. Wanted him to confide in her.

That's exactly what you shouldn't want.

"My mom's a good cook," he finally said, "but she hates having to do it because my dad's an asshole who criticizes everything she does."

Her breath stuck in her throat as she waited for him to continue. She didn't want to say something stupid and make him to stop.

"You're not eating."

Blinking at his comment, she automatically moved to open the bag and retrieve her meal before she realized that's exactly what he'd wanted her to do. She almost stuck her tongue out at him for good measure. Instead, she took the top off her dinner and began to eat, hoping he'd continue.

"My sister's a different story," he said when she'd shoved a forkful of food in her mouth. "She loves to cook. Made most of the meals when I still lived at home."

As she swallowed a bite of the best damn meatloaf in the city, her mind raced to find a question that would keep him talking.

"How's Sunny? Did she decide what she's going to do? She graduated last year, right?"

"Yeah, she did. She's still working for the vet's office. She loves animals. I want her to go to college, get a vet-tech degree, or go for a business degree and open her own pet store. I don't care. I just want her to have a degree. So she can get out."

She considered her next question carefully, went back and forth a few times before finally deciding to just ask.

"You and your dad still don't get along, do you?"

At first, she thought he wouldn't answer. And maybe that would've been the smart thing. Because she had a gut feeling this conversation could become more than either one of them had anticipated.

Or maybe Tim needed someone to talk to. And maybe she didn't want to be alone tonight. Rich's reaction to their breakup had shaken her more than she wanted to admit. She'd told the doorman not to admit Rich if he showed up, but she still had niggling worries that he'd find a way in. That he wouldn't just fade away into the background like other exes.

"That's kind of an understatement."

The hard edge underlying Tim's tone made her wanted him to talk. She wanted him to talk to *her*.

For several long seconds, she wasn't sure he would. He went silent, his gaze never leaving hers. Then he shifted deeper into the couch and the tension in her muscles relaxed, just a little.

"We don't get along, but it's more than a personality conflict. My dad's an insecure asshole who takes out his frustrations on the only people in the world who make excuses for him. When I was younger, I didn't know any better. My mom's a peacemaker, you know? Always trying to smooth things over. But as I got older, and realized he was a complete and utter prick, it got harder to keep my mouth shut. I couldn't respect a man who had no respect for anyone, and he demanded it whether he'd earned it or not."

She took a second to pick her next words carefully. They'd never really talked about this part of his life, though she'd known from RJ that Tim and his dad didn't get along.

"Sounds like a tough way to grow up."

He shrugged, his gaze never leaving hers. "It was all I knew until I was about five when my mom signed me up for hockey. My dad played in high school and a few beer leagues after. He's a carpenter, builds houses, which is a tough job in Michigan. Good pay but the window to get the job done is only a few months out of the year. Most winters, he's gone for weeks on jobs elsewhere."

"So he was gone a lot."

"Not enough, if you ask me. My mom's a medical transcriptionist so she works at home. It gave her time to run my ass around when I first started playing and then when I was playing every weekend and practicing every morning and after school. Before I signed with Barrie."

Not that she'd ever tell him, but she knew a lot about his career. She wouldn't say she'd made a hobby of it, but she ran PR for the team and he was part of the team. If *maybe* she paid a little more attention to his background than any of the other players, well, no one needed to know.

"You played your entire junior career in Barrie, right?"

His look made her wonder if he suspected her, but finally, he nodded. "Yeah. I loved it up there, was sorry to leave when I got drafted by the Colonials and sent to Reading."

He smiled and every feminine sensor in her body went on high alert. They were heading into dangerous territory when she got tongue-tied. It rarely happened. Her entire career was based on her ability to speak and to do it well. When a man tied her tongue in knots...yeah, that was a problem.

"But I've grown to love it here, too. A lot different than where I grew up."

It was on the tip of her tongue to blurt out the name of his hometown but stopped before she could.

"Do you miss your home?"

"I miss my mom and sister. I keep trying to get them to move out here with me but…" He sighed and shook his head. "She won't leave him. And I just don't get it."

"Is he physically abusive?"

Tim's gaze darkened but he shook his head. "If he'd ever hit them, I would've beat him until he couldn't move. And then I would've had the bastard put in jail. Even though my mom would've begged me not to."

Her chest tight, she had to know. "Did he hit you?"

Tim's immediate dismissal rang true. "No. He's a bully and a coward. All his shit is head games. He's just a shit human. Which you'd never know by being a casual friend."

"And your mom…"

"Doesn't believe in divorce." His words sounded forced through gritted teeth. "She's stubborn and still believes she married a decent man who needs her. I've been fighting this battle with her for years. She won't leave him. My sister won't leave my mom alone. And the vicious circle continues."

"I'm sorry." Before she realized she was going to do it, she reached out along the back of the sofa and put her hand over his, squeezing. "I can't imagine. My parents—"

"Are the ultimate perfect parents. I know."

She released his hand before she could entwine her fingers with his, which was exactly what she wanted to do. "Oh, they're not perfect. If my mom ever heard anyone call her perfect, she'd show them just how wrong they were. But they're good people. They try to make the right decisions. Sometimes they do. Sometimes they don't. But they always try."

"It's what makes your dad a good GM. He tries to do what's right for the team. I don't always agree, but then I'm just the backup goalie."

Glaring at him, she set aside the rest of her dinner. "Why do you do that?"

His eyebrows drew together, his confusion apparent. "Do what?"

"Why do you say you're 'just the backup'? Do you really not know how important you are to the team?"

He gave her that look again, the one that made her think he knew more about her feelings for him than she wanted him to. Then, after a few seconds of silence, he sighed and ran a hand through those unruly curls, shaking his head and jumbling them around a little more.

"I know my place. I know my job and I know I do my job well or I wouldn't still be here. But there's a reason I'm the backup and not the one who steps on the ice first most nights."

"But if the guys didn't know they could count on you in the clutch, they wouldn't play as well in front of you as they do. Hell, your goals against average is near the top of the league. I know you've gotten offers to play for other teams, to be the top goalie. Why haven't you taken one?"

"Wasn't the right fit at the time. The money wasn't there." He shrugged, his gaze sliding away from hers for a few seconds. "I'm happy here."

"Why?"

Damn. There went her mouth again. She probably shouldn't have asked, should've let this one go. Except...she couldn't. She wanted to know. Needed to know.

From the look on his face, she could tell he was struggling to find the right words. But she didn't need the right words. She wanted the truth.

"Because I like the people here. I like my teammates. I like my coach. I like the organization."

Something in his expression made her think he wanted to say more.

"Is that it?" she prompted.

Jesus, what was with her tonight? These weren't the questions she should be asking. Not now. Not with him here, with her, alone in her apartment. Not when his gaze remained on hers and a silence descended that became harder and harder for her to take.

Her heart had kicked up its pace again and was beating its way into her throat. They should talk about the upcoming event he was involved in.

"I told you. I like the people I work with."

Did he include her in that list? Is that what the look he was giving her meant? The two beers she'd downed certainly wanted her to believe that. Her fast-beating heart wanted to believe, as well.

"Everyone here likes you, too."

He paused. "Everyone, huh? You include yourself in that list?"

"Of course." She didn't stop to think about her answer. It was a no-brainer. Or maybe the alcohol *had* loosened her tongue. Either way, it was a truthful answer. "You're a nice guy, Tim."

She could tell by the expression on his face he'd taken her response as an insult. She certainly hadn't meant it as one. He *was* a nice guy. He was a sweet, hunky, hot, totally fuckable, nice guy she couldn't have. A guy she wanted more with each passing second. A guy she could kiss if she only closed the inches separating them and pressed her mouth against his.

Shit.

Blinking, she looked down at her hands, resting on her thighs. Okay, maybe clutching her thighs would be more accurate because all she could think about was grabbing him and yanking him right up against her mouth.

Drawing in a quick breath, she released her thighs, pushed off the couch, and headed for the kitchen. When she reached the fridge, she called over her shoulder.

"You want another beer?"

"No, thanks. I'm good."

Startled, she realized he'd followed her into the kitchen again and stood only a few inches away. Closer than they'd been on the couch. Close enough for her to want to draw in a huge breath laced with his scent.

Danger. Danger. Danger.

Staring into his eyes, she couldn't tear her gaze away. He looked straight into hers, searching for something. *What?*

"I think I better go."

It took a second for her brain to understand what he'd said. And not because she was drunk. She could hold her alcohol. No, it was how close he was and how much she wanted to kiss him. Her desire to throw herself at him made her swallow hard, her throat dry. She didn't want him to go. She wanted him to stay and...do more than kissing.

She tried to think of something, anything, to say. Well, anything that wasn't "Kiss me." Because if she said that, she wasn't sure he wouldn't take her up on it. The look in his eyes said he would.

Isn't that what you want?

"Gabby."

"Yes."

Did he hear her answer the question he hadn't asked?

She saw a muscle in his jaw jump and her gaze dropped to watch. His jaw was as rugged as the rest of him, square and covered in dark stubble, except for the area where an old scar kept the whiskers from growing. She wanted to run her fingers along the length of it, feel the stubble against her skin. Maybe against the inside of her thighs—

Blinking, she took a step back. And found herself pressed against the edge of the counter. Tim stayed where he was, but his gaze held a smoldering fire that elicited an answering warmth low in her body.

Her core clenched, and her panties would be wet in seconds. The urge to give herself permission to kiss him was a constant drumbeat in her skull.

No one would have to know.

If she asked him to, Tim wouldn't tell a soul. The man had stonewall down to an art, on and off the ice.

Could we really have this one night?

She knew the answer to that was no because she didn't want just one night. If she had, it would've been easy to find a night over the past five years and scratch that itch. Get it out of their systems.

Except she knew it wouldn't have been enough. The heat in his eyes suggested he knew exactly what she was thinking. Heart pounding against her ribs, she drew in a breath—

Tim took a step back, blinking and breaking their connection.

"I should go."

Swallowing hard, she shook her head. "You don't have to." Her brain spun like tires trying to get purchase. "We haven't had dessert yet."

His jaw clenched and the desire in his eyes smoldered hotter. The heat in her core spread outward, warming her blood and making its way through her entire body, until she wanted to fan her face, which had to be flushed by now.

"You promised me pie."

She forced the words past the lump in her throat. They sounded ridiculous. A little pathetic. But she was stupidly prepared to beg him to stay. She hoped to hell she wouldn't have to. That he'd put her out of her misery.

A split second passed that seemed like forever. She had

herself convinced he was going to turn and walk away, leaving her alone.

Instead, his lips quirked into what she thought was a grin and, finally, he nodded.

"Yes, I did." His voice, deep and strong, struck a chord low in her body. "You want it now?"

She did. She wanted the pie. She wanted him. And every second that passed, she convinced herself she could have her pie *and* her cake. Prime beefcake.

"Yes. Please."

FOUR

Tim was pretty sure Gabby had just opened a proverbial door for him to stick his size-twelve foot through.

The look in her eyes burned with a heat he'd never seen before and her body language invited him to put his hands on her. He'd never gotten the sense from her before that he'd been welcome to do it. To put his hands on her shoulders and pull her against his body. To watch her eyes as he lowered his mouth to hers, watch them flutter closed as their lips touched.

Then he'd kiss the hell out of her and deal with the consequences tomorrow. And there sure as hell would be consequences. Because of who he was and who she was.

Not that he was worrying about that now. No, he was more worried about a severe case of blue balls. Stomping down his desire for her for so long had given him a natural immunity to her. Or so he'd thought. Right now, his need for her consumed him from the inside out.

"Gabby."

Her breath hitched as he spoke her name, then she drew in a long, deep breath. Her chin came up and her lips curved with the hint of a smile.

"Pie first."

His grin widened at the implication and he caught a teasing warmth in the brightness of her eyes and the smile on her lips. Good thing she didn't know she could wrap him around her little finger with that smile.

"You wanna be civilized and use plates or you just wanna eat it out of the box?" he asked. "I got no problem with either one."

He wanted to feed her. To pick up a fork and slide it between her lips—

Argh. Just stop.

Tearing her gaze away from his, she nodded and side-stepped him on her way to the cabinet behind him.

"I'll just get some forks."

THEY WOUND up back on the couch, NHL Tonight droning away in the background. There were only two games tonight and both were on the west coast and wouldn't start until ten. She'd put them on later.

The pie sat on the cushion between them as they took turns digging in. Actually, the slice looked like half the damn pie and it was *so* good, Gabby couldn't help giving a contented sigh when they'd finally eaten it all, down to the last crumb.

"Oh my god, I think I've died and gone to heaven."

"Georgie does make the best damn pie in the tri-state area."

"Maybe in the world." Gabrielle shook her head. "I don't think I've ever had anything this good."

"I'm going to need to run a couple extra miles to get rid of the calories, but it was totally worth it."

Tim lifted a hand and rubbed it over his stomach, drawing her gaze down his body. And just like that, she was undressing him with her eyes again. Imagining what he'd look like without the t-shirt that stretched taut across his broad shoulders and the track pants that gave her a glimpse of the bulge at his crotch. Which she totally shouldn't be looking at, but now she totally was.

"Gabrielle."

His use of her full name grabbed her attention like nothing else could. It also stole the breath from her lungs and her will to deny herself the one thing she really wanted after this entire shitty day.

Him. She wanted him.

"Gabby."

Caught in his gaze, she couldn't look away.

"Are you okay?"

She wanted to scream and stomp her feet like a toddler having a temper tantrum. She didn't want to talk about how she felt. She wanted him to take her mind off what had happened, not rehash it.

"I'm fine." Getting to her feet, she grabbed the empty beer bottles off the table and headed back to the fridge. "You want another?"

He paused for a second. "No. I'm good. I'll take a glass of water instead."

This time he didn't follow her, so she had a few seconds to wrestle her emotions back under control. Her desire bubbled like acid in her veins, threatening to overwhelm her and leading to disaster.

Overdramatic much?

God, yes. Way too much. Time to act like an adult.

When she returned, she noticed he hadn't moved, except to shift in his seat to watch her.

Setting his water and her beer on the table in front of them, she eased back onto the cushion farthest from him.

And found herself sinking into his gaze. Dark and intense and filled with heat. The desire he no longer tried to hide called to her and loosened her tongue and her inhibitions. Honestly, how could she resist him? The man had been her hero today, not just once but twice. Okay, maybe doing a friend a favor by dropping off her dinner didn't count, but this afternoon, he could've walked away, minded his own business, and left her to deal with Rich herself.

"If I ask you a question, will you give me an honest answer?"

Tim didn't look surprised by her question, but he did take several long seconds to respond.

"I wouldn't lie to you."

If that had come from any other man other than her family, she'd roll her eyes. But she knew Tim. He wasn't kidding.

"Why are you here? And I'm not asking why you brought my food. I'm asking why you stayed."

Another short pause. "Do you really *not* know the answer to that?"

"I wouldn't have asked if I did."

His gaze intensified, eyes such a dark brown, they looked almost black. Such a beautiful color.

"Because I want to spend time with you. Because I've wanted to spend time with you since the first time we met. Because I can't think of anyone I want to spend more time with."

Every word struck at her heart like a tiny hammer, trying to carve out a little chink so the next one could dig deeper. Her lungs tightened until she had to tell herself to breathe. It took every ounce of her control to keep from reaching for him and dragging him close.

She could say she was shocked, but that'd be a lie. Even if she hadn't wanted to admit it, she'd known this attraction had been here for years. An attraction she'd ruthlessly ignored for her own self-preservation.

They worked for the same company, and although there was no written rule that said they couldn't be together, she'd believed a relationship between them would never work. But every one of the words he'd just said had turned a key in a lock she didn't know existed.

He'd had the courage to say those words out loud. Now she had to have the courage to make sure he hadn't said them for nothing.

"Don't say no. And don't move."

Her breathless, almost inaudible words made him suck in a breath, his chest expanding as she shifted across the cushion separating them until she was kneeling so close to him, she could feel the heat rising off his body.

"Why would I say no?"

His deep voice hit her low in her gut.

"Because I'm about to do something I shouldn't."

He shook his head slowly. "You're not gonna get a fight from me. Hell, you can tie me to the couch if you need to. I'm not going anywhere. But...I don't want you to regret whatever you're about to do in the morning."

"I won't regret a damn thing." But she needed to lay everything on the table now that she'd started. The beer with dinner had loosened her tongue and the more time she spent with him, the more she wanted to jump his bones. Literally. She wanted to climb across his lap, straddle his thighs, and take his face in her hands. Then she'd press her mouth against his and kiss him until neither of them could think straight.

Staring at him from only inches away, she couldn't wait any longer.

"The only regret I have is not doing this sooner."

Reaching for him, she cupped his jaw in her hands, his

stubble a sensual shock to her system. The warmth of his skin filtered into her body, seeping into her bloodstream like a drug. She let her fingers trail along that hard stretch while his gaze, heavy-lidded and burning, remained locked to hers.

Now that she was actually here, this close to fulfilling a fantasy she'd rarely dared to think about, she had to silence the doubts that had started to creep back in. There was no going back from this. No returning to how they were now.

You've wanted him for years. Maybe after you kiss him, you can get him out of your system.

Exactly. Sure. Right.

When he put his hands on her hips and urged her closer, she felt another layer of resistance crumble. He tugged, and she did what he wanted, inching forward until she could easily rest her hands on his shoulders.

From his jaw to his shoulders, she let her hands smooth over him, her fingers making lazy caresses all the way. Once she reached his shoulders, she spread her fingers and let them curl over the tight muscles and dip down his back.

He made a sound low in his throat that elicited goosebumps on her arms. Needy, growly. Purely masculine. Her gut drew into a tight ball, her throat dry as their gazes connected and held. She saw no hesitation, no doubt. Only desire.

She wasn't sure who moved first. In the end, it didn't matter. Their lips met, melded together with heat and want. She thought for a second that she'd be the aggressor. That he'd let her take control.

Of course she was wrong.

The second she opened to him, let his tongue invade her mouth and stroke along hers, she gave up all thought of shouldn't or should. Because this, right here, was what she'd been missing from her life.

Tim kissed her like she'd never been kissed before. And

what a sad commentary that was on her life. He kissed her like he wanted to do so much more than just kiss. His lips moved over hers with a skill that momentarily shocked her. Where had he learned to kiss like this? Like he'd been practicing all his life for just this moment.

Her muscles melted like chocolate in the hot sun, her hands going slack for several seconds before clutching at his shoulders. As rock-hard muscles flexed under her palms, her body aroused and her every nerve ending fired into almost painful attention.

Kissing him after all this time was even better than she'd allowed herself to consider. Their mouths found an immediate rhythm, her tongue dancing along his before he slid one hand to her nape, gripped her tight, and took over.

Her heart skipped a beat at the dominance in that move, in the strength in his hand and the roughness of his skin. The warmth of his body acted like an aphrodisiac, enticing her closer. She went willingly, arms wrapping around his shoulders, breasts meeting the solid wall of his chest.

She couldn't contain the low moan of excitement that rose in her throat. Or the way her nipples tightened into hard peaks. The man had muscles to spare and right now, every one of them was rock-hard. She wanted to run her hands over every inch of him, pet him until she'd gotten her fill then strip him naked.

Getting a little ahead of yourself. And what if you never get your fill?

The thought was enough to make her pause, to pull back. Tim let her go without a fight, but not without making her regret it. Her eyes blinked open, and she found him staring back at her, his gaze intensely focused and heavy-lidded.

"Gabby. You still with me?"

Was she? Sure, physically, she was fine. Except for her racing heart and starving lungs. And the ache in the pit of her stomach.

"Yes. I don't...I mean—" She sucked in a quick breath. "I didn't mean to put you on the spot like that."

One side of his mouth quirked up in an endearing grin. "I'm perfectly okay in this spot. I wouldn't want to be anywhere else right now."

Me neither.

She couldn't get the words to form on her tongue because admitting it aloud would cross a line she wasn't sure she should cross. At least, not yet.

"I think...we need to slow down."

He didn't look surprised or upset, which she took as a good sign. Her brain wasn't firing on all cylinders yet. Unlike her hormones, which were blasting off like fireworks.

"Sure. If that's what you want."

Hell, she didn't know what she wanted. Which wasn't entirely true. She knew she wanted him. She also knew if she had him, she may not want to give him up. And that would open a whole other can of worms.

Of course, the way she was straddling his lap right now, there was no easy way to extricate herself. It was going to be awkward—

Pushing his hands beneath her arms, Tim lifted her and set her beside him, as if she weighed no more than an equipment bag. Okay, one problem solved. About a million more to go.

"What's so funny?"

Tim's question made her realize she was smiling.

"Nothing." She turned to look at him, her smile widening when she found him grinning back. "Why are you smiling?"

"Because you don't have a clue what to do about this. About us. And it makes you crazy, doesn't it?"

Damn. She had to remember that Tim wasn't just another guy she could walk all over. He knew her. And he was much more intuitive than people gave him credit for. She knew a lot of people underestimated athletes. The whole dumb-jock stereotype and all that. But these guys didn't get to this level of play without being sharp. Without being able to read their opponents.

Before she could respond, he reached over and ran his thumb along her jaw, stoking that fire in her gut.

"You can't control every aspect of your life, Gabby. Sometimes, things just have to happen."

Her mouth twisted. "Usually when things just happen, they're not very good things."

Chaos wasn't good on the ice or off.

His thumb on her skin was creating all sorts of havoc deep in her body.

"Sometimes, yeah. But this... This isn't a bad thing."

It certainly didn't feel bad. She wanted to lean back into him and let him kiss her. Instead, she clenched her hands into fists on her thighs and leaned back just slightly.

"If we're going to do this, we need to think it through. Because this could get really messy."

He nodded, just a tilt of his chin. "You want to keep this between us? I'm fine with that. For now. I'm not unreasonable. I get that there are issues here. But Gabby? I'm not giving up now."

Another rush of heat, this one sizzling along all her nerve endings. "Okay. But...we need to take this slow. You're going to need to give me some space. We can't just rush ahead like teenagers."

"Fine. But I don't want you to run scared. Okay? We'll figure this out."

Her smile widened, and for the first time today, she felt like her life wasn't spiraling out of control.

"Okay. I think...I can do that."

FIVE

"Sunny, I got your message. What's up?"

Tim heard his younger sister suck in a deep breath then release it on a heavy sigh. The sound came through loud and clear on the phone, along with the emotion behind it. His gut seized. He knew exactly what that sigh meant.

His goddamn father. What the hell had he done now?

"Hey, Timmy, thanks for calling back. I'm really sorry to have to bother you, but—"

"Stop. You know you're not bothering me. Not ever. What's wrong?"

Because something was definitely wrong. Otherwise, Sunny wouldn't have called during the week. He always called home Sunday morning at ten a.m. from no matter where he was. So if Sunny was calling now...

She paused long enough to make him want to reach through the phone and pull her in for a hug. The worry in her voice made his heart hurt.

Shit. This was going to be bad.

Fifteen minutes ago, he'd taken a shower after being on the ice for a three-hour practice this morning. After he'd toweled off and pulled on clothes, he'd noticed the blinking light on his phone. It only blinked when he had a voice message. Most everyone he knew texted him if they wanted to talk to him.

But then he'd seen Sunny's number in the missed-call list. He'd dialed into his voice mailbox, phone clenched in his hand.

"Timmy, hey, it's me. I know you're really busy right now, but... Could you give me a call? I need to talk to you. If you can, call me back when you get this. Thanks. Love you."

He'd hoped the message would be from Gabby. After last night, when they'd made out like two teenagers in heat, he'd thought maybe she'd call. Just to talk. You know, like adults.

He'd told Gabby he'd give her space, but damn it, he was afraid if he gave her too much space, she'd shut down and shut him out. He'd already decided if she didn't call him by tonight, he was going to call her tomorrow and ask her out on a goddamn date. An actual get-dressed-and-go-to-dinner date.

Fuck it. He'd waited long enough. And if she turned him down again, after Monday night... Hell, he'd cross that bridge when he got to it. In the meantime, he'd thought, he'd focus on what he did best—hockey.

But this morning's practice had been a joke, at least for him. He'd let himself get caught up in the shit in his head over Gabby, and he'd missed more pucks than he'd stopped. A few of the guys had given him looks and the goalie coach had asked him if there was anything he wanted to talk about.

He'd told Coach Ellis he hadn't slept well and was fighting a headache. Maybe he bought it. Probably not, but the goalie coach was more concerned with the Colonials' number one goalie. Shane was battling a two-game losing streak that he needed to shut down quick if they wanted to make a run for the playoffs this year.

And now, he had to deal with this. He was supposed to head back to the video review room to go over tape, but he'd known that wasn't going to happen as soon as Sunny began speaking again. Because now he heard tears in her voice.

"I don't know what to do. Mom told me not to call but..."

"But what? Sunny, just spit it out."

Another sigh followed by a somewhat shaky indrawn breath.

Sonuvabitch. He was going to punch his father's face—

"Dad found Mom's stash and he freaked out. I came home in the middle of it. He looked like he was going to have a heart attack." She paused. "He started yelling and screaming about why she had so much money and where she got it and— He just seemed so angry. Mom didn't say much but that only seemed to make him even worse."

Tim closed his eyes and took a deep breath, trying to contain at least some of the burning rage in his gut. His mom's stash was the money Tim sent for her and Sunny to come visit him. Actually, he sent it so that, if something ever happened, they had enough money get away from his asshole father.

He loved his mom dearly. But he would never understand why she wouldn't leave the bastard who dominated every aspect of her life. From how much money she spent for food to what she wore to go shopping. Craig Stanton wasn't as hard on Sunny, which was the only reason Tim could think of for why Sunny continued to live at home. Tim had left when he was fifteen, so fucking happy to be out of the house. And secretly guilty because he hadn't stayed.

Sonuva-fucking-bitch.

"I'll get the first flight out tonight—"

"No." Sunny's voice had a hard edge. "No way. That's not why I'm calling. Besides, you know Mom would hate that. She didn't want me to call and I had to promise her not to. So now I've broken that promise, but I thought you should know because I'm trying to talk her into coming for a visit. A few days away. Dad's got a job in Arizona for a week. He's leaving Friday. He'll have time to cool off."

"He hasn't cooled off in thirty fucking years, Sunny. He's not cooling off now."

Shit. *Shit.* He never used that tone with his sister. He'd sworn he never would. But this crap with his dad and the situation with Gabby yesterday had made him lose his grip. That put him one step closer to being like his dad. And that wasn't going to happen. Not ever.

"Tim—"

"Hey, kid, I'm sorry. I'm not mad at you. Not at all. I'm just frustrated."

"I know, Timmy. I get it. I just...I didn't call you to make you angry or frustrated. I just want you to know we...or maybe just me...may show up on your doorstep. Like, out of the blue. And I don't want you to be a caveman and beat your chest when we get there because that won't help Mom."

"You know you're always welcome."

"Well, *if* we show up, you have to promise to act like a normal human being and not a Neanderthal. The only way you're going to get Mom to listen to you is by acting against your nature."

After a shocked second, he barked out a laugh.

"When did you become so smart, brat?"

He heard Sunny's disgusted huff through the phone. "I always have been. You just haven't been around to see it. And damn it, don't take that the wrong way."

"Nah, you're right. It's true. I got out as soon as I could."

"That was the absolute right move for you, Timmy. You and Dad..." Tim knew Sunny was shaking her head, even though he couldn't see her, "just don't get along. And you didn't abandon us, so stop beating yourself up about that. But...if I can get Mom on a plane, we're heading to you. I think they could both use a break. I just wanted to give you a heads-up."

"I still think I should fly out there and—"

"No. It's the middle of the season. You can't just put everything on hold for this. Besides, it'll just freak Mom out even more."

"I'll tell Coach I need some personal time and—"

"Tim. Stop."

The edge on his sister's voice stopped him cold. Sunny wasn't just her name. It was her disposition. He'd never heard her use that tone before.

"She doesn't need you to save her. *I* don't need you to save me. I need you to be there for us if we decide we're coming for a visit. I don't need you to fly out here and beat your chest and make things worse."

Fuck. Just...fuck.

She sighed and, in his head, he saw her so clearly, his baby sister with her straight black hair and her blue eyes and a smile that never quit.

Except now. She wasn't smiling now. And it was his fault.

"You're right. I'm sorry. I'm just worried. I don't like that you're alone out there."

"We're not alone. Jesus, you make it sound like we live outside civilization. Get a grip."

And there was the teenager he knew and loved.

"Just make the reservations," he ordered. "You've got the credit card, right? Just buy the tickets with that. Tell Mom it's my Christmas gift to you and her."

Last year, when she'd graduated from high school, he'd given his sister an AmEx with no credit limit. He'd told her to go wild and buy herself clothes, get an apartment, enroll in college, open a business. Hell, he didn't care what she did with it as long as she had the means to leave if she ever wanted to.

He thought she might have used it twice since he'd given it to her. Both times for plane tickets to visit him. And even then, she'd flown coach on the cheapest airline she could find.

"I think I can make that work," she said. "Dad was pretty sure he wasn't going to be home for the holidays. I overheard them talking about it the other day."

"Then you better text me later today and tell me you got tickets."

"You're not the boss of me."

A reluctant grin curved his lips. "And you're not too old for me to spank you."

"Which you will never do so that's a worthless threat."

Very true.

Shaking his head, he sighed. "Talk to Mom. Come out for Christmas. We'll go to New York City for a day. We'll see the tree and I'll even suffer through the Rockettes for you."

"I'll do what I can. And I'm holding you to that trip. No backing out. I love you, Timmy."

"Love you too, brat. Call me tonight, okay, and let me know what's going on."

After saying good-bye, he hung up and blew out the huge sigh that'd been building in his chest. Closing his eyes, he leaned his head back against the wall. The anger tying his gut in knots was harder to get rid of.

Every time he thought he'd gotten past this shit with his dad, something happened to make him realize he never would be.

He couldn't remember a time in his life when he and his dad weren't at each other's throats. His earliest clear memories of his dad involved a peewee game when Tim had been six. He hadn't been the best skater, but he could handle a stick, so he'd been bumped up an age level. Playing with kids who were two or three years older than him. He'd been a big kid so he'd had the advantage there.

That first game had set the tone for all the ones to follow. Tim would play. His father would berate. Luckily, his dad had traveled. A lot. Which meant he hadn't been able to get to too many games.

"Uh, hey, Tank. You okay?"

Opening his eyes, Tim caught the gaze of his youngest teammate. Nineteen and one of the best skaters Tim had ever seen on the ice, Ollie Andersen had a wild tangle of white-gold waves, freckles that made him look years younger than he really was, and amazing hazel eyes that looked like broken glass. Strangers did double takes and stopped in the middle of the sidewalk to stare at the kid. Seriously.

Ollie had been a top-ten draft pick in June and had silenced every last naysayer who'd said he wasn't ready to play in the NHL within his first two games. Just out of high school, the kid lived with the team's oldest player, Dwayne Reid, and his family. And that was a damn good thing because Ollie hadn't yet developed the thick skin needed to deal with the raft of shit professional athletes dealt with on a regular basis. He was also way too nice for his own damn good. And so fucking talented.

"Yeah, Ollie. I'm fine. You need me for something?"

"Um, well." The kid's cheeks turned a furious red. "I was wondering if we could maybe get dinner tonight? If you're busy," he rushed on, "no problem. I know you probably got things—"

"Sure, tonight's fine." Not like he had anything else to do tonight. And despite the rest of the shit in his head, Tim grinned. This kid had a way of making people do that. "You'd be doing me a favor. I was gonna grab some food and— Wait, why don't we just order in food and we can start that show you were telling me about?"

Ollie's smile threatened to crack his face in half. "Yeah, that'd be great. I think you're gonna really like it."

The kid had been talking to Tim for weeks about this show on Netflix he thought Tim would love. Some out-there, fantasy puppet show that Tim never would've considered watching. But because Ollie reminded him of Sunny, Tim knew it wouldn't be a hardship to spend a few hours watching TV with him.

Not yet old enough to go out with the younger guys who liked to the hit the clubs, Ollie and Ian Clark, one of the Colonials' prospects playing for their AHL affiliate, the Reading Redtails, hung out together when Ian happened to be in town. Otherwise, the kid spent a lot of time with Dwayne's three kids, the oldest only five years younger than Ollie.

"I'm sure I will. So what do you wanna eat tonight? Pizza or burgers?"

The kid's smile got impossibly wider. "You're gonna let me eat the good stuff? What, no salad?"

"Don't press your luck or your burger'll be made from that impossible meat shit."

Ollie's laugh rang through the hall, catching the ear of Shane and Lad, who were just coming out of the locker room.

"Tank, you are threatening to poison Ollie with fake meat." Lad shook his head, stoic expression hiding a sharp wit. "That is child abuse, yes?"

"What? They don't have vegetables in Mother Russia?" Ollie shot back.

Used to being ribbed about being Russian when he was actually Czech, Lad shrugged off Ollie's comeback.

"We only eat red meat and glass. You all are pussies eating trees and twigs."

Shane smacked Lad on the shoulder hard enough to make him pitch forward an inch or so. Lad's expression never changed.

"Maybe if you ate a few more salads, you wouldn't complain about sprints."

Tank's own grin widened. Considering Lad weighed a solid two hundred twenty pounds of finely honed muscle, Shane's observation was just a dig. Which Lad, of course, knew and shrugged off in a heartbeat.

"You are cow compared to finely honed Czech hockey machine."

Which, of course, made them all howl with laughter.

"Hey, you guys wanna watch this amazing show—oh wait." He turned with wide eyes to Tim. "I didn't mean—"

Tim grinned and shook his head. "You two wanna join the fun tonight? We're getting food."

Surprisingly, neither of the guys had plans, and since Shane's girlfriend, Bliss, was meeting friends for dinner, they both took him up on the offer.

Looked like he wouldn't be spending the night alone after all. And that was probably a good thing.

GABBY HEARD voices as she approached the hall to the locker room and stopped just before the turn.

One of those voices was Tim's. Her stomach did a little flip-flop that made her feel like she'd stepped on a roller coaster, and she took in a deep breath to stave off any additional unwanted...feelings.

Ugh.

Damn it. She wasn't ready to see him yet. Not after that make-out session last night where she'd basically thrown herself at him and tried to devour him.

She still couldn't believe she'd done it. And she knew if given another chance...she'd do the same damn thing again.

Even now, when she should be concentrating on work, all she was thinking about was how much farther she wanted to go with him. She'd had dreams all night about being naked and sweaty and under that man.

She was afraid if she had to face him now, everyone would be able to see exactly what she was thinking.

But you also have a job to do and if you avoid hockey players all day, you can't do your job.

Practical advice. Gabby prided herself on being a practical person. Sometimes, too much so. Right now, she hated it. Last night had *not* been practical. But it had been the most fun she'd had in a very long time.

Had she ever had fun with Rich? Honestly, she couldn't say she had. Kissing Rich had been okay. Sex with Rich had never been amazing, not even from the first.

Kissing Tim had left her panties soaked through. Thinking about last night made her body respond and she hadn't thought to bring an extra pair of underwear with her today. Who the hell would've thought she'd need to bring an extra pair of panties to work?

"Uh, hey, Gabrielle. You okay?"

Snapping out of her thoughts, Gabby looked up to find Riley Hatch frowning at her from the other end of the hall.

Damn. Busted.

"I'm fine. Just need to talk to RJ." She smiled at the burly defenseman. "Would you mind telling him I need to see him in my office?"

"Yeah, sure. No problem. I need a few minutes with you myself. Later's fine. Just need to talk to you about that fundraiser."

Riley's fiancée worked for one of the largest hospitals in Philly and she and Riley were doing some charity work for the hospital's Parkinson's research study. Something about patients staying active to help with the deterioration of the body from the disease. Most of the guys had pet projects. This was Riley's.

"Of course." She did a quick mental peek at her calendar. "Can we meet sometime tomorrow?"

It was Wednesday and the team had home games this Friday and Sunday, so they had some downtime before then. Next week, they had three games in Columbus, Chicago, and Minnesota. They'd leave Monday and return Sunday.

Giving her a little breathing room.

Coward.

Nah. Just cautious.

Yeah, look where cautious got you the last time.

Yes, Dating Rich had seemed like the cautious move at first.

"Yeah, sounds good. You mind if Aly joins us? Could we do it around four? She can be here by then."

"Of course. That's perfect. I'll see you then."

With a wave, Riley turned back toward the locker room, presumably to tell her brother she wanted to see him. Which meant she could head back to her office. So why was she still standing here?

She answered her own question a second later when Tim came around the corner. He didn't seem surprised to see her.

"Hey, Gabby, you got a minute?"

Be careful what you wish for.

Her lips curved into an immediate smile, unforced and totally spontaneously. Just at the sight of him. Her body responded with a surge of heat and—

Stop. Just stop.

Yes, she had a minute for him. Hell, she could have lots of minutes for him. Preferably all of them spent alone in her apartment. Forcing those thoughts out of her mind proved harder than she expected.

"Sure. Do you want to walk back to my office with me?"

His brows rose in surprise, as if he hadn't expected her to want to be alone with him. Then he nodded and caught up to her. As they walked back toward the office wing of the arena, she had to force herself not to stare up at him and drool. Drooling would definitely be bad. And embarrassing.

"What can I help you with?"

When he didn't answer right away, she glanced up to see his expression, which was much more broody than normal.

"Tim? What's wrong? Did something happen?"

He sighed, short and hard. "My sister and mom may be coming for a visit over the holidays. Just wanted to give you a heads-up."

That didn't sound bad, but the careful way he phrased his words made her pause and consider her next question carefully. Because obviously something had happened between last night when he'd told her about his mom's issues with his dad and today.

"Okay."

It was her turn to pause. With any other player, she wouldn't have pushed, wouldn't have pried. But this was Tim and, since last night, right or wrong, she felt she could ask her next question.

Stopping in the middle of the empty hallway, she put her hand on his forearm, ensuring he stopped as well. "Did something happen? Are they okay? What do you need from me?"

His expression barely changed, but it was enough to know she'd said the right thing.

Nodding, his gaze snagged on hers. "Yeah, something happened." A noise from behind them drew his attention away for a second and he frowned. "Can we talk somewhere less public?"

"Of course."

Since she didn't want to make him walk all the way back to her office on the second floor, she led him to one of the interview rooms on this floor. There'd been no press requests so the rooms were empty.

As soon as she had the door shut behind them, she leaned back against it and watched him pace. In the small room, he reminded her of a caged lion. Strongly muscled. Tightly leashed power.

When he finally stopped, he grabbed the back of one of the chairs at the small table and let his gaze lock with hers.

When he didn't say anything, she prompted him. "Do you want to tell me what's going on?"

Sighing, he shook his head, but she didn't think he was saying no to her question. So she waited.

"My sister called," he finally said, his words measured. "Told me our dad found the money I send my mom and he went ballistic."

A chill raised goosebumps all over her body. "Was anyone hurt?"

"No. My dad is a first-rate prick, a total asshole, but he's never been physically abusive. And he usually doesn't yell at them. He only ever used to yell at me."

She had so many questions but now wasn't the time. Instead, she asked, "Are you worried he's going to get physical with them?"

More head shaking. "I don't know. I just...don't know. *Fuck.* The only reason I haven't pushed harder for my mom to leave him is because he's never hit them. My dad was never warm and cuddly, and he had a mean temper, but he *never* took it out on them. Now..."

He shook his head, his knuckles white as he clenched the chair back. She wanted to lay her hands over his and interlace their fingers, try to soothe just a little bit of his anger.

"Do you know if something happened to push him over the edge?"

"Sunny didn't say. He can get mean if he's been drinking, but that doesn't happen much since I left." He took another deep breath and she could tell he was fighting the urge to rip the chair apart. He was strong enough to do it. She had no doubt. And yet, she wasn't the least bit worried about her safety. "My mom always keeps a stash hidden somewhere in the house. A can in the back of the cabinet. Somewhere my dad wouldn't think to look. Sunny didn't say how he found it, just that he had."

"Is there a reason she hides it?"

He nodded, once, just as a jerk of his head.

"A few times, before Sunny came along, he drank the grocery money. I can remember my mom crying in the kitchen, trying to figure out what she was going to feed me. I know we went to the church food kitchen a few times. I know when he found out about that, he never did it again. My mom grew up dirt poor and she knew how to stretch a dollar. I think she started putting money aside when her boss at the diner where she'd taken a second job started paying her partly in cash. She worked there part-time to pay for my hockey equipment. It was money my dad couldn't track through her pay stubs. She handed those over to him every Friday. My mom paid the bills, but my dad kept track of *everything*. If the checkbook didn't balance at the end of the month because she'd bought us a slushie, he'd bitch and moan about it for days."

Gabby couldn't imagine growing up in that environment. Someone looking over your shoulder every day, waiting for you to fuck up. She'd always known how lucky she was to have her parents; even as a teenager, when she'd probably been at her worst, she'd still loved them.

"Why does she stay?"

She wanted to take the words back as soon as they'd left her mouth. It almost sounded like she was accusing his mom of something. But she couldn't understand why a woman would tie herself to the kind of man Tim was describing.

Why did you stay with Rich even after you knew he wasn't good for you?

Good question.

Tim was silent for a few seconds, then, surprisingly, he answered.

"At first, I thought it was for Sunny and me. When I got older, I realized it just wasn't that cut-and-dried."

"Nothing ever is."

She wasn't talking only about his parents now, and he knew it. She saw his eyes narrow and darken.

He shook his head again. "No, it isn't. And I can't save her. I can't fly out there and force her to leave like some superhero in a movie. She has to want to leave."

"Do you think she might now?"

"Maybe. I'm not sure. I hope. I just...needed to tell someone." He shook his head. "No. I needed to tell you."

That lump that'd been building deep in her chest grew at least two sizes and forced its way into her throat. She tried to swallow it down, but it wouldn't budge.

"I'll do whatever you need." Luckily, her voice sounded steady. "I can talk to my dad, if you want. Warn him that you may need to take a personal leave. He won't ask too many questions if I say something."

He stood there and breathed for a few, long seconds, just looking at her. Her arms ached with the effort to keep from reaching for him. Last night had broken open a dam of feelings and right now, they all threatened to swamp her.

"I don't know. My mom won't want anyone to know her business. If she decides to come visit and someone looks at her the wrong way, she'll leave."

"Sounds like your mom's been dealing with this for a long time."

Actually, it sounded like his mom had gotten really good at hiding whatever was going on in their home and would be embarrassed if anyone found out her husband was a controlling asshole. Mentally, she shook her head at the thought, knowing it wouldn't help anyone for her to think like that.

"Yeah. And usually she had everything under control."

But this time, he was freaked out.

"Look, I know you're scheduled to start Sunday. Why don't you just give a heads-up to Coach about a possible unplanned visit from your mom and sister? I know you don't want to go into specifics, so let me help—"

"No. Thank you...but no. I'll handle it." His lips quirked up at the corners. "Can't help yourself, can you?"

Her brows drew down. "What do you mean?"

"You do know the first words out of your mouth are usually 'what do you need.'"

She shrugged. "Hazard of the job. Doesn't mean they're not sincere."

"I know that. I wasn't—" He sighed and shook his head. "You misunderstood. Never mind."

"What did I misunderstand?"

The mood shifted between one breath and the next, and the attraction that was always on simmer around him dialed up to a boil. She had no idea how he did it. Whether it was the way he looked at her or the way he leaned down just the slightest bit closer to talk to her, she didn't know.

All she did know was that she'd gone from wanting to lend a helping hand to a coworker to needing to make something better for *this* man. Wanting to do whatever he needed to lighten his burden. That kiss last night must've shaken something loose in her brain.

"I didn't mean I don't appreciate what you're trying to do. You're damn good at your job."

"I'm not offering because it's my job."

He paused, his attention honed to a laser focus. "We're heading into dangerous territory here. You know that, right?"

She did, though she wasn't sure she wanted to say it out loud. If she did, that made it real. Here, alone, just the two of them, she could pretend they weren't crossing any lines. Even though she knew they were.

She said the first words that came into her head. "I'm not sure I care."

His gaze narrowed, eyes glittering. "Dangerous words to say to me right now. Because I'm really not sure I have the willpower to deny you anything right now."

She could practically taste him on her lips, the kisses they'd shared last night a reminder that taunted her. He must have felt the same way because his jaw clenched, and she swore he leaned the tiniest bit closer before he took a step back and shook his head.

"This isn't the place for this conversation."

He was right. She *knew* he was right. She also was fast passing the point of caring.

"Come out with me tomorrow."

His low growl hit somewhere deep inside, making her core clench and heat spill through her blood.

She shook her head. "You know I don't date players. It wouldn't look right."

Even though there was no explicit rule against coworkers dating. She should know. She'd written the last round of edits to the HR policy and procedures manual herself.

"Then come over to my place and I'll make dinner."

God, yes. She wanted that so badly. She also knew it was the absolute wrong thing to do.

"We can talk about the fundraiser," he continued before she could respond. "If anyone asks, that's what we'll tell them."

You're fooling yourself. This is a date and you know it.

Right this second, she didn't give a good goddamn. She only knew she wanted to say yes.

"Gabby—"

"Okay."

Triumph. She saw it in his eyes.

Her competitive nature rose to meet it. She'd been raised by a professional athlete with two professional athletes for brothers. She knew when she was being challenged. She wondered if he'd forgotten that. She knew how to hold her own with alpha males.

"Just remember, Timothy Stanton. I'm no pushover."

His smile made a comeback and her traitorous knees nearly went weak. "This wouldn't be as much fun if you were."

"So fighting with me is fun?"

"I didn't realize we were fighting. And Gabby, anything I do with you is fun."

SIX

"Goddammit. Fuck. Fuck. And double damn fuck."

Gabby had made sure she'd closed her office door Thursday morning before going off on her mini-tirade. It was Thursday morning and she wanted to kick her damn trashcan across her room.

She was fairly decent with a soccer ball. Not as good as she was with a hockey stick, but she swore that was genetics. Right now, though, she was afraid if she took aim at the unsuspecting metal bin, she might launch it through the wall between her office and the head ticket rep's office next door.

An LA television station reporter had called with a list of questions for a story they planned to run before the Colonials home game against LA in two weeks, the first against his old team since RJ had been traded here. About RJ and the accusations. The reporter had prefaced his request by saying due to "new information," they had follow-up questions.

Gabby felt blindsided. She hadn't heard of any new information. Hell, she'd thought things had been calming down. RJ wasn't guilty. She knew that as sure as she knew her name and social security number. With a bone-deep surety. RJ would not, under any circumstances, do what he'd been accused of. Hell, most of the guys on his former team had vouched for him. Off the record, a few of the cops involved had said this would all go away.

But until it did, RJ was going to be subjected to this continuing crap.

"Shit."

She did kick the can then, literally. Not enough to send it flying but enough that it bounced off her desk and sent the few pieces of paper in there spilling out on the floor.

"Fuck."

She needed to talk to RJ. The team would be in for a late morning skate and to watch tapes in prep for tomorrow night's game. RJ would be here then.

She needed him here now, which meant she was going to have to call him in. And upset his entire day.

"Hey, Gabs, you got a min— Fuck, what's wrong?"

She felt a second's worth of remorse for the shit she was about to unload on her baby brother and, for a split second, thought she just might be able to contain it.

But as her brother's eyes widened, she realized if she didn't say something soon, her head would explode.

"Ooh, I fucking hate stupid fucking reporters." She pointed at his chest and stalked close so she could stab at him with her right index finger. "And that statement does *not* include your girlfriend so don't even start with me."

Prepared for a patented smart-ass reply from Brody, she took a breath and opened her mouth, ready to tell him to keep his mouth shut, when he closed the door behind him and crossed his arms over his chest.

"What happened? Should I go get RJ and Dad? Do you need me to do something?"

It was such a measured response, she paused, her brain trying to compute.

"Who are you and what have you done with my brother?"

Brody rolled his eyes and now he looked much more like the pain-in-the-ass she knew and loved.

"Funny. But seriously, Gabs, you look ready to stroke out. What's going on?"

Shaking her head, she sighed and turned to sink into her desk chair. "I just got a call from a TV station that wanted to ask questions about the 'new information' in RJ's case. The problem is, I haven't heard of any new information so I have no idea what we're walking into."

Brody's brows drew down as he settled onto the edge of her desk. "Shit. Have you talked to RJ yet? I haven't heard anything but then I haven't been looking. This guy didn't give you a clue?"

"No. I don't want to rile up RJ if this is just a fishing expedition. And I haven't checked Twitter yet to see what's going. Now I'm afraid to."

Brody huffed, his expression now closer to the grumpy guy he usually was. "Bullshit. You're not afraid of anything."

Totally not true, but she had to maintain some superiority over her younger sibling.

"It just caught me off guard this morning and you caught me at a bad time. I'll deal with that in few minutes. What do you need, brat?"

Only here in the privacy of her office with the door closed did she allow herself to call him by her pet nickname. He surprised her again by not bitching about it.

"It's nothing. Not when you've got this to deal with."

"Spill it. I can spin multiple plates, you know."

"Yeah, yeah. You're Wonder Woman." He shook his head.

"RJ and I were talking about what to get Mom and Dad for Christmas. We need to get this nailed down and soon."

Crap. She hadn't even thought about that yet. Her thoughts must have shone on her face because amusement spread across Brody's face with all the glee of a ten-year-old who had something to hold over an older sibling.

"Well, shit. Was that a plate I heard shattering on the floor?"

She gave Brody the finger as her mind raced. She and her brothers had a reputation to uphold with their parents' Christmas gift. They always got them the best, whether it was a trip to Paris for the Tour de France (their dad's bucket list) or two weeks in New York seeing all the shows (their mom's list) or the African safari or the Mayan ruins tour. Her dad had been especially impressed with that one.

It was something she and her brothers always did together, but this year they were getting a late start due to the cloud hanging over RJ. After sputtering for a few seconds, her brain kicked into gear and she pulled up her calendar. Christmas was a little more than three weeks away.

"Can you meet Saturday morning? We can do brunch and hash this out."

"Sure. You mind if I bring Tara? I'm sure RJ won't have anything to do. He never goes out anymore."

The look she exchanged with Brody proved they were related. She knew exactly what he was thinking because she thought the same herself. RJ had been digging himself into a burrow and that was totally unlike their brother. The guy was a pure extrovert who thrived on interaction with others. By hiding himself away, he was becoming someone they didn't know.

That had to stop. It was making him look guilty and he wasn't.

"Bring Tara. I haven't seen her for a while. You wanna meet at The Brig? If we go around ten, the first rush should be out, and the lunch rush won't have started yet. I've been craving a double order of chocolate chip and blueberry pancakes."

"I'll go wherever you say. Just tell me and I'll show up and I'll make sure RJ's there too."

"Okay. I'll text you both later to remind you."

"Sounds good. Hey, you gonna call that reporter back?"

"Of course." It wasn't like she could ignore them simply because they were asking about her brother. "You know, some people actually think it's easier to work with family."

Brody huffed out a laugh. "Those people never have. You want me to stick around for moral support?"

She wanted to wrap her arms around her brother and squeeze him before she asked what pod he'd emerged from this morning.

"No. I'm good. But thank you. I appreciate it."

They shared a smile before Brody pushed out the chair and headed for the door. "All right. Talk to you later. And try to keep that legendary cool, sis."

"When don't I?"

She muttered that under her breath as Brody disappeared, closing the door behind him. Leaving her alone with her phone and a call she really didn't want to make.

But first, she did a quick internet search. Found nothing new about RJ. Which meant whatever it was hadn't hit yet. Or the reporter was fishing. Then she called the Los Angeles law firm handling RJ's case, but no one there had heard of any "new" information being released or even gossiped about.

Looked like she was going to have to wade in blind on this one. Not exactly how she wanted to start her day.

At least she knew how it was going to end...dinner with Tim.

"OH MY GOD, you're not gonna believe this, but I convinced Mom to come for a visit. We're leaving tomorrow morning! We should be there for the game tomorrow night. Give me a call when you can. Love you. See you soon."

Standing at the stove stirring the red sauce he was making for dinner tonight, Tim grinned as his sister's message played from his phone on the counter. Finally. Some good news. This day was looking a hell of a lot better than when it'd started.

On-ice practice had been light because of the game tomorrow, but he'd put himself through a grueling workout with his trainer this afternoon, trying to work out some of the stress that'd been eating away at him since Tuesday. Starting with that scene with Gabby and her asshole boyfriend then the call from his sister yesterday...

No wonder he felt like shit today.

Yeah, I don't think stress is the reason for that tight muscle in your back.

Probably not. That one he could put down to his age. Another thing he really didn't want to think about. What he should be focusing on was the fact that Gabby would be here in less than an hour and he wanted to have dinner ready so he didn't have to screw with it while she was here.

Alone with him. In his apartment.

He couldn't believe he'd finally managed to convince her to have dinner with him, much less alone in his apartment. Especially after they'd made out like teenagers Tuesday night. He'd thought for sure Gabby's practical nature would win out and she'd cancel.

But no. She'd texted him before he left the gym to make sure they were still on. He'd wanted to reply, "Hell yes, we're still on," but figured he wouldn't press his luck.

Just the fact that she'd checked in made it easier for him to breathe.

After wiping his fingers on a towel, he picked up his phone and texted his sister to let her know he'd gotten her message and to send their flight details. He'd arrange to have them picked up at the airport and brought back to his apartment.

His mom knew his pregame routine almost as well as he did, so she knew he'd be at the arena for morning skate, then watching tape with the coaches, out to lunch with the team then back to his apartment for a nap. He'd have to be back at the arena by four so he wouldn't have a lot of time to spend with his mom and Sunny until Saturday.

Since his place had a huge guest room with its own bathroom, they didn't have to stay at a hotel. And it's not like he had a girlfriend. Although if tonight went the way he wanted...

Getting ahead of yourself, aren't you?

Yeah. But he couldn't help himself. He and Gabby had known each other for years, since the first hockey camp he and RJ had attended together as teenagers. She'd been RJ's bratty younger sister who knew the game inside and out, almost as well as Tim did. And she made sure he knew it. Some of the other guys had been intimidated by her, even though she'd been younger than most of them. Tim had been fascinated.

They'd seen each other a few other times between the time he and RJ played in the OHL and when they'd been drafted, but they'd never spent enough time together. At least, that's what Tim had thought.

Six years ago, she'd been a new hire in the Colonials PR department and he'd just been brought up from the AHL. She'd looked him straight in the eyes and told him he'd get eaten alive at this level if he didn't know what he was doing and that as the backup goalie, he had a much shorter rope than every single other guy on the team making more money than him.

Then she'd gone through the standard public relations spiel for new NHL players. He'd asked her out the second she closed her mouth. She'd raised her eyebrows, told him she wasn't interested in guys who didn't have the courtesy to listen to her when she spoke then dropped him at the locker room and left.

He was pretty sure he'd fallen in love right there. And he'd sworn, someday he'd get her to go out with him. He had a hell of a lot more patience than a lot of guys. It's what made him a damn good goalie. But it was something he'd had to work at because that's what you did to get better.

So, he'd worked at it. Slowly. He'd made a point to talk to her whenever they were in the same room. She'd told him at a team party one night that she'd been a pretty decent midget hockey player. She'd been a fast skater and a decent goal scorer but hadn't wanted to pursue it in high school. She'd wanted to concentrate on her schoolwork. She'd actually been offered a scholarship to Boston University but had turned it down to go to Temple. But she loved the game, which was why she'd wanted this job.

Usually, at team parties, they ended up together in a quiet corner, talking. He enjoyed hanging with his teammates, with a few exceptions, but he spent hours with them on planes and buses and on the ice. Sometimes, he needed a break. Sometimes, he just wanted to talk to Gabby.

Over the past six years, he'd watched her date other guys. Guys who had nothing to do with hockey. Guys who wore suits to work in downtown office buildings where they bought and sold who knew what for more money than he might ever see in a lifetime. And he was one of the highest-paid backup goalies in the league.

None of those guys had ever stuck around long. Usually because she broke up with them. She'd date a guy a few months then release him back into the wild. And Tim would clench his teeth and ask how she was doing the next time he saw her.

She'd always said fine. It hadn't worked out. They hadn't

been compatible. A couple of times, she'd just flat-out said the guy was a dick. Those were the ones Tim would've gladly punched in the face, even knowing he'd be suspended for it. Would've been worth it.

And he still hadn't asked her out. Because he knew she'd say no.

So what'd changed her mind? That make-out session? He would've thought she'd run fast and far in the opposite direction for just that reason.

Don't look a gift horse in the mouth.

The doorbell rang and adrenaline dropped into his veins like speed. His gut clenched as his heart pounded. When the fuck had he become a teenager again?

Jesus, calm the fuck down.

He finally had her exactly where he'd wanted her for years. He didn't want to fuck it up now.

Hardwood floors cool against his bare feet, he walked to the door, running a hand through his mostly dry hair before he opened the door. And nearly swallowed his tongue. Luckily, he didn't make too much of an ass out of himself by letting his mouth drop open.

Damn, she was beautiful. The most beautiful woman he knew, and he'd met his fair share of movie, TV, and rock stars who came to the games and invited the team to private parties at exclusive clubs afterward.

"Hey, come on in. Glad you could make it."

Gabby smiled and held up a bottle of wine as she stepped through the door. Closing it behind her, he couldn't resist a quick peek at her ass because, holy Christ, the woman had curves that went on forever.

When she turned, he met her gaze head on, his mouth curved in a grin that matched hers.

"Thanks for inviting me. It's nice to be out of the house and not for work. And have someone else cook." Her eyebrows rose and he could see the humorous glint in her eyes. "You *did* cook, didn't you?"

"Of course. Follow me into the kitchen and I'll prove it. Couldn't let you starve since I know you survive on takeout."

He walked by her, battling the urge to bend down and press his lips against her cheek as she huffed out a laugh. Just that soft sound was enough to make his cock twitch.

Down, boy.

He didn't want to scare her away and he didn't want to push her too far too fast.

"Pasta and red sauce okay with you?"

Tuesday night had been the first time he'd had hope that they might take this connection between them to the next level. After doing this dance for all these years, he didn't want to wait any longer. But he had to be smart. And careful. Even though the caveman inside wanted to throw her over his shoulder and toss her on his bed.

Immediately.

"Smells amazing."

He barely heard her footsteps on the soft rugs he'd covered most of the hardwood floors with. They'd been among the first purchases he'd made. Thick and soft and luxurious against his bare feet. "Oh, wait. I forgot."

"What—"

He turned to find her bent over, perfectly curved ass in the air as she removed her shoes and socks and set them beside the couch.

He practically choked on air but managed not to make a complete fool of himself by coughing.

Fuck.

She caught him looking and he thought she'd bust him about it for sure. Instead, she just gave him a look he could only describe as pure challenge. It made his breath catch in his throat and his heart pound against his ribs.

"I know you like people to take their shoes off inside."

"You don't have to."

She shrugged, still grinning. "I know. I'm more comfortable with them off. And you've got all these rugs, so..."

Good. He wanted her to be comfortable here. Wanted her to be here. A lot. Of course, he didn't say that out loud. He might not have an MBA from Wharton like some of the guys she'd dated, but he wasn't stupid.

"You wanna help me with the salad?"

"Ah. So you do have an ulterior motive. You just want me to help you make your rabbit food."

His grin returned. "Don't knock rabbit food. It's good for you. My body's a finely tuned machine. That's good, clean fuel."

Stopping on the other side of the kitchen island from him, she leaned against the marble top and grinned at him. "So is chocolate cake. You know...flour, eggs, milk. It's practically health food."

"Still got that sweet tooth."

It was one of the first things they'd realized they shared. At the first team party Tim had attended, they'd found themselves reaching for the brownies at the same time. Their hands had brushed, and they'd looked at each other and grinned.

Pretty much like they were doing now.

"You're thinking about that team party, aren't you?"

Her question twisted his guts into even more of a knot. "Yeah. You were trying to steal all the brownies."

"Oh no. I was trying to get one before the horde descended. I was surprised there were still some left by the time I got there. Especially since you'd already been there a while."

Grabbing a large bowl from beneath the island, he set it in the middle then turned to get the salad fixings from the fridge.

"We all have our vices. Chocolate is definitely one of mine."

"I know. It's one of the reasons I like you."

"So there are others?"

"Other reasons? Of course. You're tall and therefore useful to have around if I need something off the top shelf."

He grinned. "Hey, you can't blame me for that mess in your office last year. You asked me to get that box off your shelf. You didn't tell me that box held about five years' worth of paper crap."

For the next twenty minutes, they stuck to easy conversation. They made the salad. He boiled water and tossed in the fresh pasta he bought in bulk from a stand in the Reading Terminal Market because, damn, it was good.

And when they sat down to eat, they continued to pretend they were just two friends having a meal together. They talked about food and wine and movies they'd seen and every damn thing except that kiss Tuesday night.

He could live with that. For now. Because he knew, eventually, they *would* talk about it.

By the time they finished the meal and he set a plate of brownies on the table in front of the fireplace, he'd worked himself up to the conversation he really wanted to have. But he'd be damned if she didn't beat him to it.

"So," she took a deep breath, "I guess we should talk about what happened Tuesday night."

Well, hell. He hadn't expected her to jump into this conversation with both feet, but her face had that expression she got when she approached a problem. She wore it a lot more now that RJ was home.

He didn't want to add to her problems. He didn't want to *be* one of her problems.

Leaning back into the oversize chair directly across from

hers, he took a pull on his beer then set the bottle on the table next to him.

"Do you want to talk about it? Or do you just want to forget it happened?"

He readied himself for her to say, yeah, she'd rather just forget it. Then again, she could've done that in a text, and they could've gone back to their pre-kiss friendship. She could ignore the pull between them, and he could go back to wanting her and knowing he couldn't have her.

Her head tilted to the side, her expression carefully clear. "Is that what you want? To forget about it?"

He shook his head. "You should know me better than that, Gabby."

You know what I want.

He didn't say the words out loud, but they hung between them in the silence that followed. She continued to hold his gaze, hers steady, searching for an answer he wasn't sure he wanted her to find. Because if she knew how fucking much he wanted to kiss her again, she might run in the opposite direction.

"We do know each other pretty well, don't we?"

It wasn't at all what he'd expected her to say and he frowned, which made her lips curve in a grin.

"Like now." She leaned back into him. "I know exactly what you're thinking."

Was she teasing him? He'd be damned if he could tell.

"Okay, I'll take the bait." He wiped away the frown. "What am I thinking?"

Her lips quirked. "That you don't have a clue what I'm going to say."

She *was* teasing him. And because he liked it, he decided to play along.

"Isn't that the way it's supposed to be? Guys being clueless about women?"

"I guess. Sometimes." She lifted a shoulder in a careless shrug. "This is a really problematic situation."

"Are you talking about us here together tonight? Or are you talking about us working for the same team? Or the fact that your brother's my best friend and he's waist-deep in shit right now and drowning? And you're doing everything you can to make sure he doesn't go under?"

She didn't say anything right away, but her teeth caught her bottom lip and started to worry it. His gaze fell to watch for several long seconds before rising back to hers.

"You're dangerous, you know that?"

Her voice created a cascade of shivers through his body as his brow drew down. "How so?"

"You're dangerous to my peace of mind."

He shook his head. "Still not following you."

She didn't say anything right away, just stared at him, almost as if she could see inside his brain. If she could, she'd see just how much he wanted to pull her onto his lap and kiss her again. This time, though, he wouldn't want to stop at kissing.

Another sigh before she shook her head and looked away. "I shouldn't have come tonight."

He knew that's what she'd been thinking. And it made his body tense into one tight ache.

"Then why did you?"

He tried to keep the edge out of his voice, but he was pretty sure he didn't manage it entirely. Another woman might've gotten offended. Gabby just smiled at him.

"Because we're friends."

Her tone made her statement seem almost like a question. Was he supposed to answer? Probably be smart to.

"Yeah, we're friends."

But that's not all he wanted. She had to know that. Then

again, maybe she didn't. Maybe she needed him to spell it out for her. It's not like he went around declaring his love for her every day. Honestly, he'd be surprised if she knew how deep his feelings for her went. He wasn't the most emotionally available guy around. He didn't go around wearing his heart on his sleeve.

Most of the women he'd dated before would've been happy to tell her how emotionally unavailable he was.

Her smile widened. "That's good. I'm...glad we got that cleared up."

Shit. Wait a minute. "What exactly did we get cleared up?"

"That we're friends."

Aw, hell. Was she really going to friend-zone him? Again? "I didn't think there was any doubt about that. At least, I hope there wasn't any doubt about that."

Another little one-sided shrug. "You're kinda hard to read sometimes."

Now or never, asshole. Say it.

Leaning forward, he put his elbows on his knees and made sure they were eye to eye. "Then let me make my feelings totally clear." He took a breath then continued before he could think twice. "I want you. I've wanted you for years, but it never seemed like the right time to ask you out." He held up his hand to stop the words he could see forming on her lips. "Just hear me out before you start to get freaked out. Okay?"

He waited for her to think about it, saw her consider all her options before she nodded, teeth firmly lodged in her bottom lip.

Don't fuck this up.

"There's not one damn clause in my contract that says players can't date staff. I know because I looked. Twice. I under-stand why it might look bad but, frankly, I don't give a shit anymore. I know my place on the team. I will always be the backup, never the first. Hell, everyone knows I'm not that guy. I'm thirty-one years old and my career's winding down."

"No, Tim, that's—"

"Hey, I'm a realist. I may have another five years. I may blow out my ACL tomorrow and never play again. I won't regret a damn thing about my career. But I sure as hell regret never asking you out in all the time we've known each other."

She swallowed hard, her eyes slightly widened, like a deer in oncoming headlights. *Fuck.* Had he scared her off already? He gave her a little time to digest all that, wondering if she'd have something to say or if he should just keep going. Because he had a hell of lot more to say but he needed to have this cleared up first.

He was just about ready to continue when she finally responded.

"Why didn't you?"

"What? Ask you out?"

"What could you possibly have been afraid of? I've never known you to be afraid of anything."

"You don't think I'd be afraid you'd say no?"

Her head shook slowly. "I don't think you're afraid of anything."

"Maybe not on the ice. But around you..."

She let those words hang there for several long seconds. "Why? How on earth would you be afraid of me?"

"Do you *really* not know the answer to that? Come on, Gabby. You're a smart woman. You can figure that one out for yourself."

Silence descended, broken only by the soft hum of barely recognizable music coming from the speakers. He didn't recognize the song, but the low tone fit his mood of grinding desire right now.

Their gazes locked and holding, he watched her formulate

an answer. It took her several agonizing seconds, but he managed to keep his mouth shut until she finally spoke.

"I never seem to have the right answers when you're around. Any other time, I can come up with the perfect thing to say. Reporters can blindside me and I'll still be able to say the right thing. With you..."

Frustration made his jaw clench. "I don't need a perfect answer. I just need the right answer for right now."

Her lips curved with a hint of a smile. "Sometimes you say the damnedest things."

Goddamn, he loved making her smile. "Hell, sometimes I even say the right things."

She paused then took an audible deep breath. "What if I told you I only date men who *don't* remind me of you?"

Lust made his gut clench. "I'd ask what you're running from."

Blinking, she tore her gaze away from his and took a sip of her beer before she set it back down with a decisive chink.

"We've known each other a long time."

He nodded. "Yeah, we have."

"I think of us as friends."

Well, fuck. There it was. Might as well just chalk up Tuesday night's kiss to a momentary mental break and—

"But that's only because I haven't allowed myself to think of you as anything *but* a friend."

Hope rushed through his veins like acid, burning into his body as his cock thickened painfully fast. His cheeks burned and her gaze slipped from his for a second before locking back again.

"When I first started here," she said, "there was no way in hell I was going to get involved with a hockey player, especially one on my team. I already had to deal with people thinking the only reason I got my job was because of my dad. Then to be accused of screwing around with the players... I would've been roasted. And then they hired you."

His brows rose as her lips twisted into a half-hearted grimace.

"It was like the hockey gods were taunting me. And the fact that you're friends with RJ..." She shook her head. "Can you imagine what people would've said? The gossip would've been insane. But none of that meant I didn't want you."

The heat in his gut radiated south until his cock pounded against the zipper on his jeans. He wanted to shift and relieve the pressure. But he also kinda liked the bite. He played hockey. His body could take a lot of punishment.

She went quiet again and his lips parted to prompt her for more, but she leaned forward, mimicking his position. Bringing her that much closer.

"I'm still not sure this is a good idea but..." a tiny muscle in her jaw ticked, "the breakup with Rich made me realize I've been fooling myself."

He wasn't sure his voice would cooperate, but he tried anyway. "How so?"

Her gaze darkened. "I'm never going to find what I'm looking for in any of the guys I've been dating."

"Why not?"

"Because they're not you."

His hands clenched into fists as he tried not to reach across the table, pick her up, and settle her on his lap. If he did, she'd know exactly how he felt about her, and he wasn't sure that wouldn't confuse the issue even more. Because she didn't look happy about her pronouncement, while he wanted to beat his chest and roar in victory.

That was something his dad would've done. He'd seen how his father's overbearing dominance had affected his mom, how her personality had seemed to shrink until she'd become a quiet mouse who rarely stood up to the man who was supposed to be her biggest supporter.

He refused to be like his father in any way. So, no way in hell would he push Gabby into anything she didn't want or try to influence her decision in any way. She had to come to him willingly.

But it was torture to sit here and wait for her to continue.

After what seemed like a lifetime, she shook her head, her lips curving in a self-deprecating grin.

"Aren't you going to say anything?"

Nodding, he leaned forward a tiny bit more. "Yeah, I will. I just want to make sure you have your say first."

Another amused huff as the doubt cleared from her eyes. "I'm pretty sure I've never met another guy like you."

His forehead wrinkled. "How's that?"

"Most guys would be falling over themselves to convince me to get into bed with them."

Just the thought of her naked body under his while he slid inside her took his breath away. "I'm not most guys."

Her head cocked to the side. "I know that. I just... How long have we known each other?"

He frowned, not following her train of thought. "We met at the first game I played with RJ. In Michigan. So... fifteen years. You didn't want to be there, but you had some competition in Chicago, and you and your mom were gonna fly there after the game..."

He trailed off as she stood.

"What's wro—"

She came around the table then surprised the shit out of him by putting her hands on his shoulders and pushing him back into the cushions. When she put her knees on either side of his hips and lowered her ass onto his thighs, every muscle in his body seized.

"Gabby."

Looping her arms around his shoulders, she leaned forward, her nose almost touching his. He froze, waiting for her to make the next move. No way in hell did he want to do anything to screw up what he hoped would be a really good night.

"I can't believe you remember that."

"Remember what?"

His mind went totally blank as she pulled back so he could see her smile. Heat zinged through his gut, building in intensity until he thought he might melt into a puddle. Christ, he hoped like hell he didn't literally start to sweat. How fucking embarrassing would that be?

"The first time we met."

"Why wouldn't I? Wait. Don't you?"

Her smile widened. "You seemed huge at fifteen. Tall and wide and all this black hair."

She slid her hands in the hair at his nape and, holy shit, his cock pulsed like he might actually come.

"You looked pissed off most of the time and I don't think I ever saw you smile that entire time."

"I needed to nail that game for a draft spot. I had to get the hell away from my dad."

Goddammit. Why the fuck had he mentioned his dad? He expected her to draw away again, because why the hell would she want to talk about his dad here and now.

"Shit." He shook his head, carefully so he didn't dislodge her hands. "Sorry. That's not—"

"Tim. Stop." Her hands tightened in his hair, the motion more erotic now than if she'd put her hand on his cock. "I thought you were the hottest guy I'd ever seen. Of course, I was only thirteen so you were in pretty good company with Justin Timberlake."

His grin broke free. "Well, damn. Lucky me."

Her smile matched his. "You were nothing like the other hockey players I'd met before. And I grew up around hockey players. But you..."

Since he had no idea where she was going with this, he gave her a little bump with his legs. "Me what?"

"You were...interesting. Mysterious."

He snorted. "I was pissed off most of the time."

She rolled her eyes. "Don't you know that's catnip to teenage girls? I didn't think you knew or cared who I was."

"Are you serious? You were Doug Mitchell's daughter. Trust me, everyone knew who you were."

Her pout was adorable. "Nobody wanted to date me. Especially not the hockey players who hung around my brothers and my dad."

"That's because no one wanted to piss off their idol. You were totally out of my league and off limits. And you were thirteen. No one was gonna touch you."

"Yeah, I was a little slow to figure that out, but finally, when I was about fifteen, I realized why all of the hockey players I smiled at ran the other way. Until then, it put a dent in my self-confidence."

"Trust me, if you had been older, I would've asked you out."

"By that time, I probably would've said no. I gave up on hockey players by the time I was sixteen. There were other fish in the sea, and most of them had no idea who my dad was. Besides, I'd already decided I wanted to work for the NHL so there was no way I was going to date a player."

"And when you decide what you want, you get it."

Her brows arched in a way that made him wary. "Obviously, not everything."

"So what changed?"

"Are you asking me why I'm sitting on your lap right now?"

"Sure. Let's start there."

"Because I never stopped wanting you. I just convinced myself I couldn't have you."

She wanted him. Goddamn, he really wanted to believe that. But first... "And how much does this have to do with your recent breakup?"

Her fingers twisted into his hair and tugged again, causing his balls to tighten. He wasn't sure how much longer he'd be able to keep himself from leaning forward and kissing her. But he needed to hear her answer.

She didn't drop his gaze for a second. "Some. But only because I realized I kept dating guys who were so obviously wrong for me."

"Anyone who knows you could've told you that."

Another arch of her brows. "Then why didn't they? Why didn't you ask me out in any of the past five years?"

"Because you made it clear you weren't going to date hockey players. And I didn't want to get turned down by you."

"Did you want to ask me out?"

"Hell, Gabby, I told you. I've wanted to date you since the first time I met you. And when we ended up here together, I thought I'd finally get my shot. But you always had a date. Some guy with an MBA and a perfect haircut and no visible bruises."

Her laughter rang out, hitting him square in the chest, as she released one hand from his hair to stroke her fingertips along the purple skin beneath his eye.

"I think your bruises just add to your sex appeal."

His turn for his brows to arch. "Bruises are sexy?"

"Everything about you is sexy."

He'd never had a woman say anything like that to him before, and his brain stuttered for several seconds before he could think of a response. She watched him, blue eyes locked on his as he tried to figure out what to say in response. He felt he had to respond, had to say something. But what he really wanted to do was cup her face in his hands and kiss her.

For the past two days, his brain had flashed memories of Tuesday night at the worst possible moments. On the ice at practice. At the gym during workouts. Lying in bed trying to get to sleep.

But now that he had her exactly where he wanted her for the second time, he hesitated. He never hesitated on the ice. If he hesitated, he could let down his teammates and lose the game. He'd be pissed that he'd lost the game, but there was always another.

He had so much more to lose here. Couldn't make a mistake because he could lose her. And he'd just gotten her.

She's not really yours.

Then he'd have to make her his.

Unclenching his hands from the cushion, where he'd had a death grip, he lifted them to her shoulders. When she continued to stare at him and not move, he let one slide up to cup her chin while the other pressed against her back, urging her forward.

"You're the most beautiful woman I've ever known."

Her cheeks flushed with color and her lips curved a second before he tugged her forward and pressed their lips together. Like Tuesday, she tasted sweet and hot and forbidden. But now there was an added layer to their kiss. She tasted like *his*.

His lips moved against hers for long seconds before he slid his tongue into her mouth to tangle with hers. Tonight, there was no hesitation, no sense that they shouldn't be doing this. He'd had a taste of her, and he wanted more. So much more.

The hand cupping her jaw urged her to tilt just a little to the left and she obeyed without hesitation. Her easy submission fueled his already flaming desire, and in the next second, the hand on her back pressed her forward. Again, she let him do what he wanted.

And it loosened his last restraint.

Releasing her chin, he wrapped his left arm around her shoulders and his right around her lower back and pulled her tight against him. Her breasts pressed, lush and full, against his chest as her arms wrapped around his shoulders. Her tongue played with his, her hands spread against his back, her fingers digging into the muscles.

He wanted to wish away their clothes, but he didn't want to rush this. He finally had the woman of his dreams on his lap and he was going to make it last all fucking night. Even if it killed him.

Because the way Gabby was kissing him right now was pushing him hard and fast toward total meltdown. She kissed him with the same intensity as Tuesday night. Her fingers kneaded at his back, her mouth hot against his. When she scooted closer, she made him groan when she brushed against his erection. He swore he felt the heat of her core through two layers of denim.

For several long minutes, they made out like a bunch of horny teenagers, all tongues and teeth and lips and hands groping. Not a lot of finesse either. Tim would've been embarrassed at his lack of control if not for the fact that Gabby seemed to be right there with him.

When he made an attempt to pull back, simply to give them both a little breather, she followed him, her hands pulling them back together. He let her, at least for a few seconds, before he lifted his head and held her at bay.

Her eyes opened, barely, and the look she gave him was pure frustration. It made him want to bare his teeth in a predator's grin.

"What's wrong?"

She sounded like a grumpy child who'd had her favorite toy taken away. He liked it. A lot.

"Nothing's wrong." He ran a hand over her hair, the silky strands gliding through his fingers before he released them. "You're so damn pretty."

She smiled, heat and something sweet that made his gut clench.

"Thank you. Now why don't you take off your clothes so I can put my hands all over your body?"

He nearly choked on his next breath.

"Holy shit. Do you want me to come in my jeans?"

Her expression got a whole lot more serious. "No. Absolutely not. I want you to come inside me."

He couldn't believe he was about to ask this question, but he had to hear her say it.

"Gabby. Are you sure? We can't go back from this."

Her gaze never wavered. "I told you we waited long enough."

"Nothing's changed."

"I've changed. And I'm tired of waiting for you."

She leaned forward and sealed their mouths together again. This time, he felt the determination in her kiss. She wanted him and she wasn't going to let anything stand in her way. Not even him.

Which was absolutely fine because he wanted her. Maybe even more than she realized. And now that she'd given him permission...

He pulled back. "Take off your shirt. If I do it, I might rip it off."

She blinked and froze for a split second.

Shit. What—

Then her lips curved, and that smile felt like a caress against every part of his body, but especially his cock.

"And if I tell you to do it yourself, what are you going to do?"

HARD LINES & GOAL LINES   111

He'd rarely seen this side of Gabby. Christ, it was fucking hot. The girl he'd first met had been a little wild, a little haughty, and a whole lot of devil-may-care. The woman she'd become had lost that wild side. Or so he'd thought.

Apparently, she'd been hiding it and only allowed it out in private. He was okay with that, as long as it was only around him. He didn't say that. He really wasn't that stupid. Instead, he grabbed her hips and yanked her forward without warning.

She gasped in surprise but began to chuckle a second later. That cut off when he pulled her shirt out of her jeans and stripped it over her head. His gaze dropped to take in what he'd bared, and now his lungs felt like they'd been filled with cement and his cock had turned to stone. Living, painful stone.

A purple lace bra cupped full breasts, straining against their confinement. His mouth started to water, and he swallowed hard. Looking up, he caught her gaze and held it as he lifted his hands and filled his palms with her soft flesh.

Her eyes closed as he kneaded her, not hard enough to hurt but hard enough to make her moan. He expected to hear a hell of a lot more of that all night long. Her nipples poked through the lace and against his palms, so he rubbed them, eliciting another yearning sound from deep in her throat. She swayed forward, her lips brushing against his, but he pulled away, causing her to open her eyes.

"I want to watch while I touch you. You don't know how many nights I jerked off thinking about you." His voice was barely understandable, nearly a growl. "Now I want to see you."

"Why did you never say anything?"

He rubbed his thumbs over her nipples, considered ignoring her question to put his mouth over them, but figured she deserved an answer.

"Because you would've shut me down."

He leaned forward and put his mouth on her neck, tasting

her smooth, warm skin with a flick of his tongue. Shuddering against him, she put her hands on his shoulders, squeezing hard.

"You're right. But at this moment, I have no idea why I would've done that."

Stringing a line of kisses along her neck, he bit her at the curve to her shoulder before continuing on his way. He wanted to taste every inch of her skin, make her limp in his arms before he got his cock anywhere near her. Because he had the feeling once he got inside her, he wouldn't last more than a minute. If he was lucky.

Even though, right now, he was feeling really fucking lucky.

Working his way back to her neck, he licked the hollow of her throat and continued on to her other shoulder. Gabby tilted her head to give him more access, a small sign of submission that made his hands tighten.

Her back arched, pressing her breasts more fully into his palms. At the same time, she scooted forward, the seam of her jeans pressing against his zipper, causing his hips to rise and press his cock against her mound.

Nipping at her shoulder, he drew back and looked down at her. Her eyes were slitted but glittering, her expression infused with lust. He couldn't wait to see her after he'd made her come while she was spread out naked on his bed.

Getting ahead of yourself, aren't you?

He hoped like hell he wasn't. She seemed as fully committed to this as he was, but if she said stop, he'd stop. He'd just have to make sure he never gave her a reason to want to leave. Because he had the one woman he wanted to spend the rest of his life with in his arms.

Not that he was going to say that now. He knew better than to spill his guts. It was too damn soon. But he wasn't going to be able to hide his overwhelming feelings for her for long. And he didn't want to. Every kiss he pressed against her skin was his promise. A promise to do his absolute best to drive her out of her mind and satisfy her every desire.

"You need to behave."

Her gaze held heat and challenge.

"I thought that was the point. To misbehave."

"It is. But if you go full-on bad girl, you might give me a heart attack."

"Maybe you need to see I'm not the person you think I am."

He heard something in her tone that made him pause and consider his next words carefully.

"I know who you are, Gabby."

She shook her head, her lips curved in a rueful grin. "Maybe. I hope you do. I hope you're not disappointed if you find out you don't. Not really."

Releasing her breasts, he cupped her face in his hands and pulled her forward for a kiss. He opened his mouth over hers and kissed her deep, showing her just how much he desired her. When he pulled back, he grinned, pretty damn pleased with himself. It took several long seconds for her to open her eyes and she needed to take several deep breaths before she did.

Her gaze stayed unfocused for a bit before she blinked.

"The only thing that would disappoint me is if I do something to make you want to leave."

Her hands made a lazy trek back to his head, where she scraped her nails along his scalp before tugging on his over-long hair.

"I'm not sure you could right now. I can't believe you still don't know how much I want you. Guess I'm just going to have to show you."

She slid off his lap and onto her knees on the floor before he realized what she was doing. But when her hands reached for the button on his jeans, the air in his lungs left in a rush.

She kept her eyes locked on his as she tugged the button

through his jeans, her fingers making fast work of it before sliding her hands up his stomach, nails raking across his skin. He bit back a groan as an electric shock zapped through him, starting in his balls.

"I never took you for a tease."

"Oh, I'm just getting started. I have years of pent-up fantasies."

"You're not the only one."

"I might let you have a few of them." She made a little shrugging motion. "Then again, I might be greedy and take what I want."

Raking her nails back down his stomach, she stopped just short of his waistband. His abs contracted and her gaze shifted down. The smile that kicked up the corners of her mouth threatened his sanity.

"Right now, I'm going to be greedy."

"I'm good with that."

Her smile widened and an avalanche of lust practically blinded him. He wanted to reach for her and pull her back up so he could kiss her. But he also wanted to see what she'd do, left to her own devices. The thrill of anticipation tightened around his lungs and made it insanely hard to breathe.

Then she stole his breath completely.

Rising up onto her knees, she scooted forward, forcing him to spread his legs wider for her to get closer. Her hands smoothed up his sides as her lips moved closer and closer to his stomach. To just above his waistband, to be precise. He could feel her breath against his skin and his abs tightened until he thought they would fucking snap. His heart pounded until he thought it'd bruise against his ribs.

He dug his fingers into the cushions, not caring if he ripped the damn things to pieces. He only cared—

Her mouth landed on the taut skin just below his belly

button, sending an electric shock through his body. Groaning, he let his head dip back as she brushed her lips against that skin then began to kiss her way up his body. Her hands aided and abetted, twisting his nipples as her lips stopped midway there.

Opening his eyes, though he couldn't remember closing them, he found her staring up at him.

"Still with me?"

Her voice dug deep into him, breaking another piece of his control. "Yeah. But you're gonna need to move a little faster."

"Why's that?"

"Because if you don't, you're gonna find yourself on your back on the floor."

"Are you going to be on top of me?"

"Absolutely."

Her eyes held a wealth of mischief. "Do your worst."

She lowered her lips to his chest as her hands glided down his body to his jeans. Tugging on his zipper, she lowered it tooth by tooth, giving his cock momentary relief from its confinement. But when she slid one hand inside his jeans to grip his cock through his boxer shorts, he reached his breaking point.

"Don't say I didn't warn you."

She paused, her head popping up to look at him, and he pounced. He moved with a speed she wasn't expecting, startling a squeak out of her before as he grabbed her off the floor, scooped her into his arms, and headed for his bedroom.

"I thought you were taking me to the floor."

Her words registered a second before she nipped his neck, just below his ear.

"I'm too fucking old for the floor. And we have a game tomorrow."

The words were out of his mouth before he realized that probably wasn't the right thing to say to a woman. She probably didn't want him to be thinking of anything but her.

Then again...

"Damn right, you have a game tomorrow. No wild monkey sex. We need you healthy if we're going to make the playoffs."

He stopped in the center of the living room, the door to his bedroom in sight, and started to laugh.

"What's so funny?"

Luckily, Gabby didn't sound upset. She sounded amused.

"I think you're probably the only woman I know who'd tell me I need to be careful not to injure myself during sex."

Her lips twitched for a second before she started to smile.

"Okay. I'll give you that one."

"Oh, you're gonna give me a hell of a lot more than one."

He got his feet moving again as she huffed out a laugh. Which died the second her back hit the bed and he came down over her, sealing their mouths together in a kiss that demanded everything she had.

He had one purpose now, and that was to make her come. Hell, it could be the only purpose in his life. At least, for the next several hours.

Coming up onto his knees, he stripped off the rest of her clothes. Her tight jeans gave him a little struggle, but he never gave up.

"Couldn't wear sweats, could you?"

"Wouldn't want to make it too easy for you."

Finally tugging her jeans down her legs, he tossed them over his shoulder as she fell back, a challenge in her smile that he saw briefly before his gaze dropped to her breasts. Encased in that sexy lace bra.

"Fuck, Gabby. That's hot as hell. You're leaving that on."

"But—"

She groaned as he put his mouth over one nipple, sucking the hard tip between his teeth and biting down until she squirmed.

"Tim."

Her voice had a needy quality that lit a spark in his gut and made his balls tight. He liked it. A lot. So he switched sides and she did it again. He spent the next several minutes making her writhe just with his mouth on her breasts, suckling her through the lace.

When she put her hands on his shoulders and shoved him away, he went, but only to move his mouth down her torso. He kissed straight down to the waistband of her panties, which matched the bra.

He ran a finger around the top. "These are coming off."

"First take off your pants."

"Nope."

"Why not?"

"Because if I do that, I'm not sure I can make you come before I get inside you."

It was dark in his bedroom, but he was pretty sure she just blushed. He swore he could feel the heat of it rise from her skin.

"You just have to put your hands on me and I'm nearly there."

"Damn. Guess I'll have to put that to the test."

"Tim—"

She gasped as he slid a hand beneath her panties from the top, skimming over the short hair on her mound to the smooth lips of her pussy, already slick and hot. Sealing his mouth over hers, he kissed her hard and deep as his thumb found her clit and he pushed two fingers inside her sex to stroke the delicate tissues there.

Groaning into his mouth, she arched up, pressing her lower body closer, forcing his fingers deeper.

He stroked her a few times, feeling her muscles tighten around him. Her hands gripped his shoulders, nails digging into the skin while he fucked her with his fingers. Slowly. When he felt her get close, he'd slow and withdraw completely. After a few minutes, she moaned and twisted her head to break the kiss. He let her but only because he wanted to know what she had to say.

When he opened his eyes, they'd adjusted to the dark and he saw frustration clearly on her face. He grinned.

"You're a fucking tease, Timothy Stanton. If you don't make me come—"

He slid his fingers back inside with more force, watching her eyes close as she wriggled against his thumb. A flick of his thumb and her back bowed off the bed, her sex clenching around him as she came.

He drew it out as long as he could, stroked her until she shoved at his shoulders and he slid his fingers from her body. He let his gaze rake down her body, so fucking turned on by the lacy lingerie and the sprawl of her long legs and all that naked, warm, sleek skin.

Leaning forward, he put his mouth on her neck just below her left ear and began to kiss his way down her body. He tried not to miss a single inch. But he only got as far as her belly button before she sat up and took him down to the bed on his back.

Truth be told, he let her do it, willing to give her whatever she wanted.

"Take off the rest of your clothes now. I want to ride you."

Oh hell yes. He was absolutely okay with that.

Sitting up, he stripped off his jeans, boxers, and socks and dropped them. But he didn't sit back right away. Gabby placed a line of kisses across his shoulders, delicate brushes of her lips that sensitized every inch of flesh on his body. Her fingertips feathered along his spine, goosebumps spreading like wildfire.

Eyes closed, he sank into the sensation, into the desire and the heat and the knowledge that the woman he'd wanted for years was finally in his bed. He wasn't expecting her to swing around his body, straddle his hips, and shove him down onto his back. Staring up at her with a grin curving his lips, he bent his arms beneath his head.

"And I want to see you. Turn on a light."

"Bossy."

"You should know that about me already."

"I do."

Twisting his upper body, he reached for the bedside table and flipped on the lamp. The low, soft light made her skin glow.

"Good idea." He grinned up at her. "Now about that ride..."

Her eyebrows rose. "Maybe I want to torture you a little."

"Do your worst, hon."

Lifting her hands, she gripped his shoulders. Expecting her to lean forward and kiss him, he tilted his chin back. Instead, she raked her nails down his torso. The sensation was sensual torture. Goosebumps covered his entire body and his cock responded as if she'd sucked him into her mouth. He drew in a short, sharp breath, his body going rigid.

"Jesus, Gabby."

Her smile held a wicked edge. "Aw, big, tough hockey player." She scratched low across his abdomen, carefully avoiding touching his cock. "Can't take a little tease."

This side of Gabby fascinated him. Playful. A little softer. The no-nonsense woman who ruled the team's public persona with an iron fist was nothing like this smiling, teasing, sexy woman who was going to drive him insane with lust.

And he was totally okay with that.

"I can take anything you can dish out."

"Glad to hear it. Now lie back and take it like a man."

He burst out laughing, making her smile wider. Until she wrapped one hand around his cock. His laughter cut off as quickly as it started while her lips curved in a seductive smile that promised all sorts of pleasure.

"Amazing how quiet a man can get when you've got your hand wrapped around his cock."

"You want me to talk? I can do that. You can touch me anywhere you want, as long as you keep your hands on me. Stroke me. Kiss me. Fuck me. Whatever you want."

She leaned forward and kissed him, hand still on his cock as her mouth moved on his, tongue dancing along his, demanding more. His hands fastened onto her hips, yanking her down until he felt the warmth of her core against his abs.

With a soft moan, Gabby shifted her hips, rubbing her labia cross the tip of his cock. His hips lifted into hers, nudging at her opening before slipping just inside. They were perfectly aligned before he realized—

"Hang on. Let me grab—"

Reaching out one hand, he fumbled open the bedside table drawer and grabbed a condom, which she plucked out of his hands before pressing a line of kisses down his center until just before she reached his cock.

"You know I'd never put you in any kind of danger."

Her lopsided smile as she stared up at him made his cock bob.

"I know."

Then she put her mouth on his cock and blew his mind. His head dropped back into the pillows and his hands slid up her body to rest on her shoulders. She took him right to the edge then backed off, her lips and tongue even more torturous than her nails had been.

Fast losing himself in the heat of her mouth and the suction of her lips, he pressed on her shoulders to get her to back off. She did, but only after one long drag on his cock.

Rising up onto her knees, she opened the condom and rolled

it down his erection, her light touch another form of torture before she pulled away to sit back and look down at him.

"I never realized you were so mean." He practically growled as he waited for her to move. "Come on, Gabby. Take me."

With her burning gaze locked on his, she planted one hand on his ribs, used the other to pull his cock away from his stomach. Then she sank down, engulfing him in heat.

He sucked in a deep breath but she didn't let him catch it. She began a hard rhythm that forced him to respond, to snap his hips up to meet hers and drive his cock as deep inside her as he could get.

Her head dropped back, her body sleekly feminine and beautifully curved. Just looking at her riding him pushed him closer to an orgasm that threatened to break him. His hands found their way to her hips and slowly, he took over the rhythm. Which meant faster. Harder. More.

"Tim."

His name on her lips in that husky low voice flicked a switch inside him. Wrapping his arms around her waist, he pulled her down to meet his lips and thrust, feeling her break and convulse around him just before he came with a groan, pulsing inside her.

SEVEN

Gabby's eyes snapped open when she felt the bed move as Tim shifted closer.

She'd known she wasn't in her own bed the second she woke. She knew that because there was a large, hard, hot body wrapped around her and one of Tim's huge hands spread over her stomach, making her core clench.

Good morning to you, too.

She didn't want to move and dislodge his hand. Hell, she didn't want to move at all. She wanted to stay here as long as possible and soak up his warmth. And relive last night. If she closed her eyes, she could feel him moving inside her, the thick length of his cock spreading her wide. She'd loved every fucking second of it.

She wanted a repeat right now. Her body flushed with heat just thinking about it. Her lungs stuttered and fought to pull in air. If she wasn't careful, she'd roll over, push Tim onto his back, and climb on top of him. He probably wouldn't care but she had to be in the office by nine. That meant she needed to get her ass in the shower and get ready for work.

Stealing a glance at the clock, she groaned when she realized it was almost eight a.m. But then she remembered it was a game day. She didn't have to be in until noon.

Rolling over and climbing on top of Tim was looking better every second.

As if he'd read her mind, Tim tightened his arm and tugged her even closer. Her ass nestled against his erection, the heat of his body searing her back. She felt content. Secure. Horny. But like all players, Tim had a game-day routine and she didn't want to mess with it. She just wanted to mess with him.

"Morning. You hungry?"

She smiled, realizing the morning after with Tim wasn't going to be awkward, like it had been with almost every other man she'd been with. They'd slept together but they'd also known each other for years. There was already a comfort level between them.

"Yes, I am. You going to feed me before I have to go get ready for work?"

"Of course. Game day."

And that was all he needed to say.

"Hope you're okay with bacon, eggs, and pancakes."

"Maybe just one of those for me. When do your mom and sister get in?"

"You worried about being caught?"

Was she? Maybe a little.

"No, I just don't want your mom to think..."

"What? That we're adults who have sex?"

She elbowed him, gently.

His laugh rumbled against her back. "Anyway, you've already met my mom."

"Yes, but not while I was naked and after I just had sex with her son."

He nuzzled his nose into her hair. "We haven't technically just had sex. They should be here around noon, depending on traffic. Oh, hey, I know you're usually busy during the game, but do you think you could spend a little time with my mom? She's not really used to big cities and I'm afraid all those people might freak her out."

The damn man was downright adorable. "Do you think she'd be more comfortable in the suite? She'd be out of the crowds and my mom's gonna be at the game tonight. I'm sure she'd love to have your mom and sister join her."

"You sure that'll be okay? I'm not looking for special treatment—"

"You're not getting special treatment. Mom and Dad invite players' parents to the suite all the time. Besides, our parents know each other. If my mom knew your mom was going to be there, she'd insist your mom join her anyway."

"That'd be great. Thanks. I really appreciate it."

"Do you think your mom'll remember me? I can't remember the last time I saw her. Has she been here to see a game?"

"Yeah, she and my dad came to one game my first season. It didn't go well."

The wry tone of his voice gave her pause but she didn't want to censor herself every time he mentioned his dad. "Can I ask what happened?"

She felt him shrug. "Usual bullshit. We got into it, and he's never been back. Which meant my mom's only been to a few of my games. Which sucks."

"You're close with your mom, aren't you?"

"Yeah. Even though..."

When he didn't continue, she turned and laid her cheek on his chest, right over his heart. "Even though what?"

"I don't know why she stays with him."

She paused, trying to phrase her question carefully. She'd known Tim for fifteen years, had secretly adored him for most of those years. But last night had changed everything and now she didn't know if she should ask such a personal question. Then again, she'd slept with him. That should give her a little latitude.

"Is he really that bad?"

Tim didn't answer right away, but he'd lifted his hand to stroke her hair, lulling her into an almost boneless state of being. Finally, he took a breath.

"Mostly to me. Yeah. I know some of it's perception on my part, but...he can be an absolute asshole. I have no idea what my mom ever saw in him. Maybe he wasn't always an asshole. I don't know. But for as long as I can remember, he's just been a dick."

"To you."

"Yeah. My sister can do no wrong. And I'm okay with that. Sunny's always been this sweet kid with a big smile and a huge heart. I can be a pain in the ass. But my dad and I... We're like oil and water. Or fire and gasoline. I can't remember a time that we didn't fight. It's always something. I talked too much, or I didn't talk enough. I was always home. Then I was never home. I didn't practice enough. I practiced too much. I wasn't good enough."

She gave her next sentence serious thought before speaking. "You know you're never going to please him, right? People like that... They just aren't ever going to be satisfied."

Rich had been like that.

The hand resting against her back began a slow stroke up and down. This must be what a cat felt like when being petted. She wanted to lie here forever and let him stroke her until all her bones felt like mush.

"It took me years, but yeah. I figured that out around the time I was thirteen or fourteen. It took me until I was almost sixteen, right before I left for the OHL, to realize I no longer cared. And I told him that before I left. That was the worst I ever saw him. It was the first time I think I realized how much we antagonized each other. I mean, he got angry at my mom but never in the same way. And he adores Sunny."

"Sounds like his problem is only with you."

"That's why I left the first chance I could. I figured, at least, there'd be less friction between him and my mom."

"Did he see you play in Barrie?"

"Twice. I think. Maybe."

"Twice? That's it? What about your peewee games?"

"My mom was at almost every game, unless Sunny had something. But by the time she started to play field hockey in junior high, I was already gone so Mom didn't have to worry about choosing between us."

"Did your dad play?"

"A little. Yeah. Never really good at it."

"Maybe he was jealous? I've seen it happen before."

"Don't know. Don't care. That relationship is never going to be fixed. I have no respect for him, and he's made it pretty damn clear how he feels about me."

"So it doesn't bother you anymore?"

He went silent for several long seconds. "Honestly...no. I have my mom and my sister and as long as they think I'm okay, I don't give a shit what he thinks."

"I think you're a pretty decent guy, too. I always have."

Oh god. That sounded so stupid. She wanted to take the words back as soon as they'd left her mouth. But when he lifted her chin to get her to look up at him, he was grinning. Which made her smile.

"Good to know, especially considering the circumstances. I'm glad you don't think I'm an asshole."

With a sigh, she maneuvered until she had her arms draped across his chest and her chin resting on her hands. He reached to brush her hair back from her face, her heart melting just a little more at the tender way he did it. Like he was afraid he'd be too rough with her.

Of course, this was a guy who had to take ninety-mile-an-hour shots and bounce back up from collisions with two-hundred-pound men. He was rock solid and tough as granite. And looking at her like she was the most desirable woman in the world. Maybe it was time for Tim to prove just how much stamina he really had.

"Definitely not an asshole." Moving her hands, she pressed a kiss against his chest, felt his muscles tense. "Tough." Another kiss, closer to his right nipple. "Strong."

Pushing up onto her hands, she resettled her body over his, her knees on either side of his hips, hands just above his shoulders. Beneath the covers, the heat of his body soaked into hers, making her wet and achy and horny as hell.

Every breath laced with his scent hit her system like high-octane aphrodisiac. She wanted to run her tongue along his neck and taste him. Then run her tongue down the center of his body and take his cock in her mouth and suck him until he groaned in surrender.

Now that she'd had a taste of him, she wanted to devour him, gorge on him. Tie him to the bed and make him her slave. She thought he might allow her to tie him down, but she wasn't sure he'd ever be her slave. The man liked to be in control. She didn't think he'd ever be able to give up that much of himself.

But if she wasn't careful, she could become addicted to him.

Right now, though, she wasn't going to worry about any of that. The only thing she was going to worry about was making him groan again like he had earlier.

She flicked her tongue at his nipple, heard him growl as his hands tightened in her hair. Why did she love having his hands in her hair? There was just something so sensual about it.

"Fuck, Gabby."

Fierce urgency took hold as she moved her hands to his shoulders, holding him down before opening her mouth over his left nipple and using her teeth to nip at him. Not hard enough to hurt, just enough to know she wasn't playing. She was deadly serious and ready to take what she wanted.

***

"TIMMY! Honey, I'm so happy to see you. It feels like it's been forever."

"Hey, Mom. I'm glad you're here. Sorry I couldn't meet you at the airport."

Returning his mom's tight hug carefully, he pulled back with a grin. He wasn't about to mention the fact that it'd been almost a year since he'd seen her. Didn't want her to think he was throwing it in her face.

Drawing back, he took a good look. Next to him, his mom looked small and fragile. In reality, she was five-seven, thin but toned from a daily regimen of running and yoga, her hair a shade between dirty blonde and red-gold, and her eyes the exact same blue he saw in his own mirror every morning.

Other than their eyes, they looked nothing alike. Tim had sometimes wondered if she looked at him and saw his father. It was one of the many reasons he tried so hard not to be anything like him. Right now, the only thing he saw in her eyes besides happiness was fatigue, probably from the pills she took for her anxiety over flying. Otherwise, she didn't look any worse for wear.

"Of course, you couldn't. We totally understand you have a game tonight. Which is why your sister and I are going to stay out of your hair today. We know you have a routine and we don't want to mess with that."

"Yeah, you're an old man. Set in your ways. I know you need your nap before a game."

Turning with a grin, he grabbed his sister and pulled her into a tight hug, holding her until she started to squirm.

"You're not too big to put in time-out."

Sunny's laughter matched her hair, bright and wild, her copper curls contained now in two braids that hung to the middle of her back. She looked twelve, not two months shy of twenty-one. And was practically a carbon copy of their mom.

"You'd have to catch me first and you're not as fast as you used to be."

Probably more true than she knew. "How was your flight?"

"Mom only thought we were going to die once so it was pretty good."

They shared a smile as their mom rolled her eyes. "I'll admit I have a little fear of flying, but so do millions of other people. Now, why don't you show us around and we'll get settled in while you take your nap. You start tonight, right? What time do you have to be at the arena?"

"I need to be there by five for dinner, but I can skip and we can—"

"No." His mom's firm response took him back to his childhood. Before his dad had gotten worse and his mom had become even more quiet than she'd always been. "Sunny and I will be fine on our own tonight."

"But—"

"Dude." Sunny laughed. "Mom's got it all thought out. Don't even think of messing with her plan. We're gonna have dinner at that restaurant you're always talking about then we're gonna go to the game and then we figured we'd go out and hit a few clubs and party the night away."

Tim and his mom exchanged a grin at that one. They all knew that'd never happen. Samantha Stanton wasn't a clubs-

and-party kinda person. That's what Tim had gotten from his mom. Her introvert nature. Sunny, however...

"Uh-huh. How about you guys wait for me after the game and I can bring you back here. Tomorrow, I've got plans so be prepared. Gabby got you tickets for the owners' suite and—"

"Do you mean Gabrielle Mitchell?"

His mom's gaze narrowed and the look she gave him made him feel like a teenager who got caught sneaking into his room after being out with his friends all night. Like maybe she knew something.

"Yeah. Why?"

"Oh, nothing." She shrugged but her expression made him pause.

"Is there a problem?"

"No, of course not." She waved away his concern. "I always liked Gabrielle. I mean, I don't know her well, but she always seemed nice. I just know you've always had a thing for her so—"

"Whoa. Wait. What?"

His mom rolled her eyes. "Oh please. Of course you do."

Her voice held so much conviction, he was momentarily struck dumb.

Shit. Seriously? What the hell?

A quick look at his sister confirmed his worst fears. Sunny thought the same thing.

"Dude, did you think we didn't know?" Sunny's expression was filled with sibling mockery, including rolled eyes. "Seriously. She's the only girl you ever even mention. I kinda wondered for a while if you had a boyfriend and just didn't want to say anything. Which would be totally okay. But then you started mentioning Gabby and, well..." She shrugged. "We just took it from there."

He wanted to deny, deny, deny but he didn't want to lie.

Not to his mom and sister. But he also didn't want to talk about something that was so new. And uncertain.

"Oh, don't look so shocked, hon." His mom reached over and pressed her hand against his cheek, smiling her mom smile that made him feel about five years old. "You do realize you never talked about any girl, right? Not ever. Not even as a kid. It was always hockey or your friends or what was happening at school or what tv show you were watching. I mean, I assumed you were dating but whenever I brought it up, you brushed me off."

Well, shit. He'd never given his mom and sister enough credit. "I guess...I never dated anyone I wanted to introduce to you."

"So are you now?"

Sunny's sly grin had him reaching over to tug on a braid. "Nosy."

"No. Well, okay, yeah, but only because I love you. You deserve to be with someone who makes you happy. Someone to lighten you up a little."

"Are you trying to tell me I'm a lead balloon?"

"No. Of course not." Sunny's smile softened. "I just think you're a great guy and you deserve an equally great partner. But if she treats you badly, just let me know. I have ways to make her pay."

Laughing, he shook his head. "Should I be worried about you taking me out while I sleep?"

"Of course. It'll keep you on your toes."

He had a feeling by the end of this weekend, he'd be a fucking ballet dancer.

EIGHT

Nervous anticipation had started churning in Gabby's stomach sometime around five.

She told herself it was something she ate or just her worry over RJ. But by six o'clock, she finally stopped lying to herself.

It was totally because she was about to meet Tim's mom and sister. Which was ridiculous. She'd met Samantha and Sunny before. Sure, it'd been years ago, and she barely remembered, but she met players' families all the time. No big deal.

Except...this was. At least for her. And not just because she was sleeping with Tim. Or not sleeping, which was more the truth. A hell of a lot of *not* sleeping.

She'd met the parents of other men she'd slept with before. But none of them had made her feel like this. By the time she took the elevator down to the main concourse to meet Samantha and Sunny Stanton, her palms were sweaty and she could barely stand still.

She tried to remember the last time she'd seen Tim's mom and vaguely remembered a thin, strawberry blonde who'd been kind but quiet. As she stepped out of the elevator and into the lobby for the private suites, she immediately picked out Tim's family in the small group of people milling around.

Actually, it was his sister who was easy to pick out, with her bright red hair, which meant the older woman standing with her who looked just like her must be Samantha. They stood a little apart from the others, although, as Gabby watched, she saw Riley Hatch's girlfriend, Aly Martin, approach them with a smile, quickly followed by Bliss Vescovi, goalie Shane Conrad's fiancée.

As Aly held out her hand to Sunny, Suki Williams' one-year-old daughter made a dash for Samantha and attached herself to her legs. By the time Gabby made it across the room to them, Samantha had picked up Coco and was letting the little girl play with the bracelet on her wrist.

A few of the other wives and girlfriends were milling around, chatting before heading up to the WAGS lounge. She smiled at them as she passed but didn't stop to talk, as she might have done another night. She knew all of them by name and had a good relationship with almost all of them. There were a couple girlfriends who didn't fit in or didn't care for the hierarchy of the hockey wives, but Suki, as the oldest and wife of one of the assistant captains, did a good job of keeping the younger ones in line and showing them the ropes.

As the daughter of an NHL player, Gabby knew how hard this life could be on players' significant others. Outsiders thought the life of an NHL wife was all privilege and leisure. The ones who were only in it for the fame and money found out pretty quickly that for nine months out of the year, their lives revolved around their boyfriend/husband's hockey schedule. Their days were ruled by workout schedules and practices and game-day routines and weeklong road trips. If they had kids, the women were practically single parents from September through

April. And if the team made it through the playoffs, they could be playing through mid-June.

Sure, those two months from the end of June through the end of August were filled with vacations in exotic locations and intensive one-on-one time with their guys, but she knew a lot of women who couldn't handle the life. Several of the most stable marriages throughout the league were couples who'd been high school sweethearts. Like Colin and Suki. And Gabby's parents. Being a hockey wife wasn't for the faint of heart.

Her cheeks heated as she remembered Tim talking about meeting her for the first time as kids. Then seeing her again when they'd started working together here. She hoped Tim's mom attributed her pink cheeks to being out of breath.

"Mrs. Stanton, hi, I'm Gabrielle Mitchell."

Samantha looked up and met Gabby's smile with her own. "Hello, Gabrielle. It's so nice to see you again. Thank you so much for having us in the team suite."

It was on the tip of her tongue to say she did this for all the parents, but that wouldn't be true. Most times, she got however many tickets a player needed for the lower bowl and never gave it another thought. Sometimes, if it was a special occasion or the parents had some connection to the team, Gabby would get the okay to invite them to the suite.

This time, there'd been no question. Gabby's mother had made the final determination.

"Of course, Samantha and Sunny will sit with us. It'll be nice to catch up. We haven't seen each other for a few years."

"It's nice to see you, too." She turned to Sunny and held out her hand, which Tim's sister took. "And you must be Sunny. Tim talks about you all the time."

The younger woman laughed. "I'm almost afraid to ask what he says. I love my brother, but he can be a jerk."

"Sunny! Don't say that about Tim." Samantha rolled her eyes, shaking her head but laughing. "I'm so sorry. My children are heathens, apparently."

Suki laughed as she reached for her daughter, now squirming in Samantha's arms. "That's not totally true. I can tell you Tim is wonderful with Coco. He's even babysat for us. Twice. But don't tell him I told you. I don't think he likes people to know he has a soft side."

Wow. Another tidbit about Tim to sock away in her memory. She'd had no idea. Then again, she'd deliberately not been keeping tabs on him before Wednesday. Funny how your entire life could turn on a dime. Or a kiss.

"Oh, my Timmy's always been a marshmallow."

"Yeah, a marshmallow that's been held over the fire too long."

The women all laughed at Sunny's wry comment before Gabby began to hustle them all toward the elevator. The conversation muted a little as they rode up together. Suki and the other wives and girlfriends split off for the family lounge at the opposite end of the hall. The women would head out to their seats in the arena after they'd caught up for a half hour or so while Gabby led Sunny and Samantha to the owners' suite, where her mom was waiting.

As expected, her mom greeted Samantha like she was an old friend. Which was probably pretty close to the truth. Samantha's face lit up when she saw Gabby's mom, and their conversation took off. As mothers with NHL player sons, they had a lot in common.

And so did Sunny and Gabby.

She turned to find Sunny studying her intently. Not hostile, just...curious. Gabby smiled and took a few steps closer.

"So...you and Tim, huh?"

Gabby froze for one long second as she stared back at Sunny. Her immediate response was to deny, deny, deny. But she didn't want to lie to Tim's sister. So she gave her next words a few extra seconds of thought, while Sunny's smile grew.

"Tim and I have been friends for a long time."

Which made Sunny's smile widen even more.

"Yeah, I know." Sunny moved closer, probably so their moms wouldn't overhear. "He talks about you. And by talks, I mean he mentions you occasionally. You know Tim." She rolled her eyes, which made Gabby bite back a grin. "It's like pulling teeth to get him to say more than a few words at a time."

Gabby thought back to last night when he'd had more than a few things to say, but wisely kept her mouth shut.

"But he actually talks about you sometimes. And he's never mentioned another woman. I mean, like, never. Mom and I wondered if he was gay." She shrugged. "Wouldn't matter to us but it would explain why he's never talked about anyone he was dating. I can't imagine he's been celibate for all these years. That'd just be gross."

Coughing to hide a laugh, Gabby shook her head. "I know Tim's dated."

Just never the same woman for more than a couple of months. Actually, he'd gained a reputation as a recluse. But she wasn't going to pass on gossip to his teenage sister. Especially not about Tim's sex life. And most especially not when Gabby *was* his sex life.

Sunny's gaze narrowed, as if she could read Gabby's mind. "Do you know who?"

"I don't think I'm the person you should be asking that question."

"You really think Tim's going to answer?"

"I think your brother's love life is his business."

Okay, that was almost an outright lie because she totally thought his love life was her business right now. At least, she wanted it to be her business. And *only* her business.

Sunny's expression made Gabby feel like she'd accidentally exposed a secret. "And I think you're really good at talking about a subject until the other person gives up in frustration."

Sunny laughed, her expression so adorable Gabby couldn't help but smile back at her.

"I like you. I think you and I are going to get along just fine because I think we know exactly what Tim needs and won't stop prodding him until he gets it."

"Your brother loves you very much, you know."

Gabby didn't know why those words were the ones that came out of her mouth next, but she knew they were the *right* words.

Sunny's laughter dissolved but her smile widened as she lifted a shoulder in lazy agreement. "I know. He never lets me forget it."

And that was a very good thing. When Tim decided you were his, he made sure you knew it. Gabby had realized that soon after she'd woken up this morning.

"Gabby, please don't let Sunny monopolize you all night." Samantha came from behind Gabby to put her arm around her daughter's shoulders. "I know you have work to do, and this girl will talk all night if you let her."

Sunny looked at Gabby with a smile that let Gabby know Sunny wasn't going to tell her mother what they'd been talking about. It'd be their secret.

Gabby smiled back.

"It's no problem. Really. But I do have rounds to make, so I'm going to leave you with my mom for now. Enjoy the game. I'll be back sometime in the third quarter."

Gabby waved and headed out of the suite with a smile.

———

"TIMMY! Oh my god, you were great tonight! Who knew you could hold up a bench that well!"

Laughing, Tim caught his sister in a bear hug as she threw herself at him. His mom and Sunny were waiting in the hall down from the locker room, along with the other team family members. He took a quick look around to see if Gabby was anywhere in sight and tried not to be disappointed when she wasn't.

"You're hell on my ego, kid. You can stay home Sunday."

"Sunny, stop tormenting your brother." His mom turned her smile on him. "I'm looking forward to seeing you play, but it was nice to watch a game where I wasn't worried about you every second."

His mom reached out for her hug and let him squeeze her tight for a few seconds before pulling back to check him over. He hadn't been in goal, but his mom never not checked him for injuries. He'd gotten used to it years ago, but it was strange to have her here to do it after being apart for so long.

"You can criticize me Sunday. I'm set to play then."

His mom's smile lit up and Sunny clapped her hands excitedly.

"Wow, they really do pay you to play."

Tugging on his sister's hair, he put an arm around both of them and started walking toward the exit.

"You ready to head back to my place?"

"Actually," his mom patted his back, "Gabby's mom invited us to join them at a hotel downtown for dessert. Unless you're tired and want to get home."

Surprise made him stop in the middle of the hall and stare down at his mom. "You want to go?"

"Yes, she does," Sunny piped up. "And so do I. It's Friday and we're here to have fun. I think Mrs. Mitchell said Gabby will be there, too."

The smug expression on his sister's face told him much more than the innocent tone of her voice.

Biting back a sigh, he shook his head at her. But he wasn't about to turn down an opportunity to spend time with Gabby, especially not when he wasn't sure when he'd see her again outside of work. With his mom and sister staying with him for at least the next four weeks, he would either have to confess and tell his mom and Sunny that there was something going on or he and Gabby would have to get sneaky.

Now, no one would ever accuse him of being brilliant because, until his sister and mom had arrived, he hadn't considered what having them stay with him would do to his sex life. Of course, before they'd told him they were coming, he hadn't had a sex life.

Besides, one night didn't exactly make a sex life. But he'd be damned if he let it stop at one night. Guess he'd be getting acquainted with that cat Gabby said she had—

Someone smacked him on the back and Tim turned to see RJ smiling at his mom.

"Oh, we're definitely going to have some fun. Hello, Mrs. Mitchell, it's nice to see you again."

RJ came up beside them, a welcoming smile for Sunny and Samantha making the guy look like he was in a fucking tooth-paste commercial.

Sunny's eyes widened so much, Tim had to cover his grin with a cough. He'd be sure to use her obvious infatuation against her when they were alone. Anyway, she was too damn young for the guy.

"RJ, how are you? It's been years. It's so nice to see you again."

As his mom and RJ held a short conversation to catch up, Tim watched his mom. She actually looked happy. Her smile didn't look forced and her shoulders weren't hunched like she had the weight of the world on them. She even looked years younger than he remembered seeing her. Or maybe that was just perception.

Whatever was causing it, he didn't care. She looked happier than he'd seen her in years. Which wasn't saying much, because he'd seen her so rarely over the past three years.

And there was that damn guilt again, making his gut clench. He shook it off and, after a few more minutes of talk, got everyone moving toward the garage, where they all agreed to head straight to the hotel restaurant where Mrs. Mitchell had reserved a room.

On the drive, his sister and mom kept a running conversation about the game. Both were almost as knowledgeable about hockey as he was. Sunny surprised him with a deeper understanding of the game than he would've expected, laughing at him when he mentioned it.

"Dude, when guys find out your brother's an NHL player, they like to brag about how much they know about the sport. Most of them don't have a clue. If I know more than they do, I don't want to know them. They're just assholes."

"Sunny. Language."

He and Sunny exchanged a grin in the rearview over their mom's admonishment.

"Sorry, Mom. They're douchebags."

It was their mom's turn to roll her eyes. "Yes, they probably are. And you definitely don't need to date a douchebag." She paused and looked up at Tim. "Speaking of dating, are you seeing anyone right now? I only ask because I don't want to cramp your style while we're visiting. Sunny and I can always stay at a hote—"

"You're staying at my place. And no, you're not cramping my style."

From the backseat, Sunny made a point of clearing her throat, which made their mom turn to look at her before stopping to stare at Tim.

Traffic on Broad Street was a mess, so he couldn't take his attention away from the road. But he knew if he didn't say anything, his mom would interrogate Sunny and his sister wouldn't keep her mouth shut.

"Are you dating someone right now?"

He could honestly answer that one. "No. I've gone out with a few women over the past few months, but I've been busy with work."

"You know you're not getting any younger, honey. Don't you think it's time to settle down?"

Now Sunny started to laugh as Tim shook his head.

"Yeah, Tim, why *don't* you find a nice girl and settle down?"

"Did I invite you two to visit just so you could harass me?"

It was so good to hear his mom and sister laughing, it was definitely worth the possibility of his relationship with Gabby being discovered.

And from Sunny's knowing looks, she already had her suspicions. Which would probably be confirmed the second he and Gabby were in the same room together.

Do you care?

Honestly? No. Unless Gabby did. Then he'd do whatever she wanted.

Arriving at the restaurant a few minutes later, a hostess led them to a private room in the back, where Gabby and her mom stood talking to another woman Tim didn't recognize. Gabby's back was to the door, so she didn't immediately notice their arrival. But her mom did. She waved and motioned them over.

Gabby turned and caught his gaze. And he figured anyone who saw the smile on his face had them figured out in a heartbeat. Gabby's own smile was more restrained but the heat in her eyes... Yeah, it was there.

So what the hell were they going to do about this?

NINE

"Can I talk to you for a second? I've got a question I need you to answer."

Gabby looked up into Tim's eyes, her heart doing that little stutter that happened way too much when he was around. You'd think she was a teenager being asked out by Justin Timberlake. Or whoever teenagers thought was hot right now.

They'd kept their distance so far, not making it obvious that they were trying not to talk, and probably making it totally obvious that there was something going on between them.

Still, there wasn't much they could do about it. Eventually someone would figure it out and then everyone would know.

And when they did?

It would be a relief. Because even though they'd only spent one night together, she wanted a hell of a lot more and she was getting close to the point where she didn't care what anyone else thought. Amazing how that had happened over the course of a day.

Her normal practicality deserted her whenever Tim was around.

"Of course." She turned to her brother Brody's girlfriend,

whom she'd been talking to for the last few minutes. "Excuse me, Tara."

Tara nodded, her assessing gaze going from Tim back to Gabby. If it'd been any other reporter, Gabby would've made more of an effort to hide her feelings. But she'd known Tara long enough now that she trusted her implicitly. She also considered Tara a friend.

"No problem." Tara's lips curved in a smile that said Gabby would be facing a few more questions later. "I'll just go see what Brody's up to."

"Why don't we go in the hall for a few seconds." Tim's voice caressed her from the inside out. "Quieter out there."

And no one could overhear them.

She followed him with a nod, trying not to look guilty as hell as they walked through the door. She didn't look back. Didn't want to know if anyone was watching them slip away like secret lovers. Which they totally were.

Tim stopped several feet away from the door, where they could still hear the low hum of conversation from the crowd gathered there, but no one should be able to hear them. Her parents had invited a few other people to this impromptu gathering, including Dwayne Reid and his wife and Ollie Andersen, the youngest player on the team, who'd only just turned nineteen. He and Sunny had broken off a little while ago, though Gabby didn't think Ollie had much to say. He'd pretty much stared at Sunny the whole time. Sunny had talked enough for the two of them.

Which couldn't be said for Sunny's older brother. Tim didn't say anything as Gabby stared up at him, standing close enough that all she had to do was lift her lips and he could bend down and kiss her. Which she totally wanted him to do. Right now.

His eyes narrowed and she wondered if he could read her

mind. And maybe he could because he leaned down. Her breath caught in her throat as his lips stopped a hair's breadth from hers.

"This is going to suck."

She smiled as he pulled back, though she was disappointed when he didn't follow through on that kiss. Even though she knew they shouldn't. Anyone could walk out at any time.

And would it be awful for people to know?

"What's going to suck?"

His gaze remained on her mouth, making her heart race. "Well, my mom and sister are here for the next month, at least. I'm glad to have them but...bad timing." He lifted one hand and let his thumb barely graze her chin, sending a shiver through her that she didn't bother to hide. "I want to spend the night in a bed with you."

His voice lowered even further until it barely registered as sound. She still heard every word.

"I'd say come over after they go to bed tomorrow night, but you have a game Sunday. And you start."

His lips kicked up at the corners. "If anyone else said that, I'd think they were trying to blow me off."

She rolled her eyes. "You know I'm not."

"Yeah, I do." He bent his head a little closer, barely enough to make a difference. Definitely not close enough. "We could skip out now for a quickie in the bathroom. Do you think anyone would miss us?"

She had to work hard not to laugh too loudly. "Yes, I think they would. Especially Sunny. She knows about us, by the way. Did you say anything to her?"

"No, I didn't. She's just too smart for her own good. But she won't say anything to anyone else. She'll just torment me."

"I like her. She's sweet."

"And nothing like me, huh?"

"You're sweet in your own way."

"I'm really not, but you can think that if you want." His gaze dipped to her lips again for a few brief, searing seconds. "So, I promised Sunny I'd take her to New York to see the Rockettes. I was thinking maybe we'd go up on the twenty-third. Wanna come?"

Yes sprang immediately to her tongue but she bit it back. She wanted to go, wanted to spend the time with him because he wanted her to go. But...

"Your mom and Sunny probably don't want me to tag—"

"Trust me. They will *not* be upset if you come with us. But I'll understand if you don't want to publicize our...relationship. Yet."

Yes, she should care how it would look for her to go on a trip with Tim and his family. Her job was all about optics, and that optic was definitely not the image she should be projecting. But she might have a solution for that.

"Would you mind if I brought my mom, too? I know that's a huge imposition—"

"Hell no. That's a great idea. I don't know why I didn't think of it. Definitely. Ask your mom."

Her smile couldn't be contained, and his gaze narrowed, got more intense. Which wiped away her smile and made it much, much harder to breathe. Her nipples tightened, her lungs expanded, and her core clenched.

"Fuck it."

He muttered the words under his breath, and it was all the warning she got. He leaned closer and covered her mouth with his, sealing their lips together and stealing every last shred of her common sense.

Not caring if anyone saw them, she wrapped her arms around his shoulders and pulled him closer, going on tiptoe to press her breasts against his chest.

Tim groaned, his arms crushing her against him and sliding his tongue between her teeth to tease her tongue into playing with his. She never forgot that they were standing outside a dining room, where almost anyone would walk by and see them. Right now, she didn't care. Not one damn bit.

Obviously Tim felt the same because his hands moved to her hips and he lifted her until her feet left the floor and she had to tighten her arms around him.

Time spun out until finally, some noise from inside the dining room caught her attention and she drew back reluctantly. Tim let her go, but not without a final kiss that left her wanting so much more.

"Not fair."

Those two words did not in any way express her level of frustration. His smile had a wicked curve that made her want to repeat that kiss, except this time they wouldn't stop until they were naked. And probably arrested for public nudity.

"What's not fair is that I have a hard-on and you can walk back into the room like nothing happened."

She couldn't help herself. She looked down. Her turn to grin at him.

"Now that's playing dirty."

His voice lowered to a growl, making her thighs clench. She was going to need to change her panties when she got home. She'd much rather have him take them off.

"We should go back in."

He nodded. "You go ahead. I'll be there in a few seconds."

She felt stupid, leaving him in the hall and slinking away like they were doing something wrong. They weren't. She just wasn't sure what they were doing.

"Tim..."

"Unless the next words out of your mouth are 'please fuck me against this wall,' I don't want to hear them."

An image of him doing just that flashed in her brain and she could barely breathe. "You play dirty."

"Only with you. You like it."

No reason to lie. "I do."

He lifted a hand to brush back the few strands of hair he'd mussed earlier.

"Good. I'll call you later tonight when we're both alone."

"I'll be waiting."

She finally got her legs moving.

"I'll be fucking aching."

She hoped she had her smile under control by the time she walked back into the dining room.

"SO YOU GONNA TELL us what's going on with you and Tim, or you just gonna front like nothing's happening?"

Since Gabby had been expecting the question, she was prepared Saturday morning when RJ asked her at brunch. Sitting across the booth, RJ stared at her with raised eyebrows, looking like he expected her to be surprised.

"No, I'm not. Now, we need to figure out what we're going to get Mom and Dad for Christmas. We're really late this year and—"

"Wait. Gabby and *Tim*?" Brody stared at her like she'd grown another head before he looked at RJ. "Seriously?"

RJ snorted. "What? You didn't notice they both disappeared from the restaurant at the same time last night? I mean, they tried to play it off like nothing happened but..."

Brody's face screwed up in a frown. "Damn. How'd I miss that? Yeah, well, I guess it makes sense. They've always had a thing for each other."

"I know, right?" RJ nodded at Brody. "Can't believe it's taken them this long."

With a sigh, Gabby crossed her arms over her chest and glared at Brody as she shoved her elbow in RJ's side. Her cheeks burned and she knew if she didn't shut them down soon, it'd devolve into a battle of two against one and her brothers would harass her until they got an answer out of her.

"I don't know what you're talking about." Oh hell, she didn't even sound convincing to herself. "Now, if you two are finished gossiping, maybe we can figure out what we're doing for Mom and Dad this year."

"Umm, have you met your brothers?" Tara grinned from across the table. "I swear all they do is gossip. They're like teenage girls. But this time, they're kinda right. I'm not sure everyone noticed, but...I'm pretty sure everyone noticed."

Gabby rolled her eyes. "Damn it, Tara. Not you, too. Why are you siding with them? We women need to stick together or these idiots will run right over us."

Tara laughed, loud enough to be heard outside the damn restaurant. "You know, speaking as a reporter, you pretty much just admitted your guilt."

"I'm not guilty of anything."

"Yeah, that pretty much seals the deal." RJ nodded, a natural grin finally curving his lips. "Hey, I think it's a good thing. You and Tim have been circling each other for years."

"We have not. I have no idea what you're talking about."

"For a PR hack," Brody lifted his arms in defense of her swat across the table for the little-brother dig, "you suck as a liar. Come on, Gabs. You can admit it to us. We're family. We love you. We won't give you shit for this." He paused. "Well, not a lot of shit, anyway."

Shaking her head, Gabby considered her options. On one hand, they were right. Who could she trust if not her brothers?

And she had the utmost faith in Tara not to spill the beans. True, she was a reporter, but Tara had the strong code of ethics most reporters lived and died by.

"Okay. Maybe, *maybe*," she held up her index finger in front of RJ's mouth when he opened it, "Tim and I have...explored the possibility of a relationship."

And each other's bodies for several hours. But her brothers didn't need to know that.

"But..." and now she sighed, knowing if she admitted this, she couldn't put the genie back in the bottle, "he's still a member of the team and I'm not sure... It's just complicated."

She saw a smart-ass comment forming on Brody's lips, but before he could really piss her off, RJ put his arm around her shoulders and squeezed her tight. Smiling up at him, she leaned her head on his shoulder, appreciating how seriously RJ took his role of big brother. Even now, with all the issues he was having with the rumors and lies flying in California, he was still there for her and Brody. She knew it as sure as she knew the sun would rise that he wasn't guilty of any of the charges those assholes in California threw at him.

"It doesn't have to be. I think you're making it more compli-cated than it has to be. He's wanted to ask you out for years, but he knew you'd never agree while he played for the team. So what changed?"

She didn't want to tell them what had happened with Rich, didn't want them to know she'd been so stupid to date a guy like him. Neither of her brothers had ever liked him, which should've been a big, glowing thumbs-down sign. Instead, she'd let herself be talked into going out with him. Rich had been the "safe" option. Until he hadn't been.

She was worried that if she told her brothers, they'd be incredibly pissed off and decide to teach Rich a lesson. Rich would never be able to defend himself against two hockey players who worked out on a daily basis and could hold their own in a fight against the league's toughest goons. Of course, if they dared to so much as touch him, Rich would charge them with battery and neither of them could afford that.

"Gabby?" Brody's gaze had narrowed. "Did something happen? Is something else going on? What—"

"No. No, there's nothing else going on." At least, nothing she wanted to tell them. "I just...I think maybe we just got tired of waiting."

Tara snorted. "So you've been hot for this guy for years and never did anything about it?" She shook her head, her eyebrows arched in disbelief. "You've got way more restraint than I do."

Brody wrapped his arm around Tara's shoulders. "You just knew you didn't want to lose a good thing when you found it."

Brody's shit-eating grin made everyone around the table groan, except for Tara, who threw her balled-up napkin in his face.

Shaking her head at them, Gabby let her gaze narrow.

"You know I think Tim's one of the best guys in the world." RJ's lips held a grin, but his eyes were deadly serious. "Neither of you are getting any younger. If you can find some happiness, I say go for it."

———

"HEY. Sorry to call so late but—"

"No, no. I'm glad you did. I'm not asleep. It's only... Oh shit, well, I guess it is kinda late. You start tomorrow. What are you still doing up?"

Tim grinned at Gabby's response as he sprawled out on his bed. "I was hoping I'd get to see you today but Sunny and my mom wanted to go sightseeing. We did the whole deal. Walk, bus, walk some more. I didn't realize every single house in

Society Hill had a history that our guide had to tell us all about."

Her soft laughter made his cock stir. He didn't bother to will his hard-on away. He'd known he'd have one just hearing her voice.

"Sounds like you had a good time."

"I did. It was great spending time with them but...I was kind of hoping I'd get to see you today."

She paused long enough that he began to worry. Then she sighed so loudly he heard her through the phone.

"I know. Me too. But I'm glad you called. I was going to call you earlier but..."

"But what?"

"But I wasn't sure I should. I mean... I need to know what we're doing."

"What do you want us to be doing?"

"I don't... I'm not sure."

"Well, I am. I know exactly what I want. You."

"Tim—"

"No, wait. Just listen."

He wasn't sure but he thought he heard a smile in her voice. "Okay."

"If we were together right now, I'd be throwing you on the nearest flat surface and following you down. I'd kiss you until neither of us could breathe and then I'd strip you naked and use my mouth all over your body. I'd wait until you were begging me and I literally couldn't take another second and then I'd spread your legs and slide my cock inside you and fuck you until neither of us could see straight."

The silence from the other end of the line was deafening.

Shit. You fucking idiot. Why the fuck—

"Is that a promise?"

He sucked in a deep breath. "Do you need it to be? Because then yes, absolutely."

"I'm going to hold you to that the next time I see you."

"What about Monday night? I think Mom and Sunny will be okay if I take the night off."

Her soft laughter made him burn from the inside out. "You know they're adults and you're not babysitting, right?"

Wincing, he shrugged, even though he knew she couldn't see it. "Yeah, I know. I just don't want them to feel like I'm ignoring them."

"I'm sure they don't. But I'll understand if you don't want to—"

"Stop. I want to do anything with you. Hell, I'll sit through endless hours of torture if it means I get to be with you. It's not that. It's just..."

He wasn't sure how to put his feelings into words that wouldn't make him sound like a giant asshole who thought the world revolved around him.

"You don't want your mom and sister to feel like you abandoned them so you could get laid?"

He laughed, a little startled and a whole lot amused by her dry tone. "Yeah, I guess you could put it that way."

"I'm willing to wait for whenever you have the time. I'm not going anywhere."

No, she wasn't going anywhere. But would he?

The thought hit him from out of nowhere, random and earth-shaking. What happened if he was traded? If they didn't renew his contract? Did he even want to sign with another team?

"Tim?"

"Yeah. I'm here. And no, I don't plan on going anywhere either."

Her turn to pause. "I know that's not a guarantee. I know

life is unpredictable, especially in our business. But... I want to try."

"Then we'll make it work."

"So confident."

"Occupational hazard."

"Definitely one of the things I like about you."

"Good to know there's more than one."

He'd meant to make her laugh. Instead she went silent for a few seconds. And when she spoke, his cock went from half hard to fully erect in seconds.

"Oh, there are so many more than just one. I like the way you look at me. I like the way you kiss me. I like the way you listen to me when I talk. I love running my fingers through your hair. And down your back. And the way you respond when I run my nails along your cock."

She'd stolen all the air from his lungs and his chest was so tight he thought his ribs might crack.

"I'm going to make you pay for that."

"Promise?"

"Damn right."

He didn't want to hang up but he really should get to sleep.

"See you after the game?"

"Of course."

"Talk to you then."

"Night."

"Good night, Tim. Sleep well."

At least he'd go to sleep with a smile on his face.

TEN

"Good game, Tank."

"Woulda lost it without you."

"Good job."

Tim acknowledged every compliment from his teammates before they left the ice with a nod and a tap of helmets, but he knew the praise wasn't warranted.

They'd won, but it hadn't been pretty. If only a couple of bounces of the puck had gone the wrong way, they would've lost to the worst team in the league. Boston was having an awful year, but the Colonials could've easily lost the game if not for Boston's two hottest players being on the IR.

After saluting the fans, who were even cheering half-heartedly, Tim waited at the gate to the bench as the rest of the team filed down the hall to the locker room. As an assistant captain, RJ was the last man. He slapped Tim on the back before following him off the ice.

"You saved our asses tonight, Tank."

"No, I really didn't. But thanks for the ego stroke."

"Whoa. Hey, you okay?"

Stopping before they entered the subdued chaos of the locker room after a game, Tim pushed up his mask and nodded. "I'm fine. Just not happy with how I played."

"Well, you should be. We won. And you were a big part of why we won. What's wrong with that?"

"Nothing. It's just me being stupid. I'm fine."

"I've known you a long time. I've never seen you like this."

"I'm fine."

"Then prove it." RJ leaned in to make sure no one else could hear them. "You need to go in there and act like we had a fucking great game. You're a goddamn hero right now because that last save handed us the game. Act like it."

Tim was grinning by the time RJ finished his little speech. "Why the hell aren't you wearing the 'C' yet? Hell, I'm gonna start an 'RJ for captain' campaign."

Sighing, RJ shook his head. "I'm not sure I want that damn letter on my sweater right now."

"That's bullshit. No one else dared to talk to me like this. And you're right. I need to do exactly what you just said. Because the team needs to see it. They need to know I'm not falling apart on them. And you knew that. Like I said...captain."

RJ shook his head, but he'd started to grin as well. "You're a dick. How the hell'd you turn that around on me?"

"Guess I'm just that good."

RJ didn't speak for a few seconds. "You are. Even if you don't believe it all the time."

"You don't want to hug me, do you?"

"Only if you let me kiss you, too."

Tim laughed and RJ stepped out of the way so he could enter the locker room and tell his teammates what they needed to hear.

KNOCKING ON GABBY'S DOOR, Tim rolled his neck, trying to work out some lingering stiffness and trying not to let his restlessness show.

He'd called her a half hour ago, just after his mom and sister had declared they were taking Tim's car and heading to the King of Prussia Mall for some mother-daughter retail therapy. Sunny had taken great pains to tell him they wouldn't be back until at least ten o'clock. And then they'd probably go right to bed so if he "wanted to, you know, like, be somewhere else," as Sunny had so delicately put it, she and their mom wouldn't "notice."

They knew exactly what he was going to do the second they left. Which was probably why they'd told him they didn't need him to drive. He'd offered. They'd declined.

Thank God. If there was one thing he did not want to do on a Monday afternoon in December, it was fight the crowds at the mall. Just thinking about it made his jaw ache. He couldn't imagine his mom would love it, either. Then again, she spent most of her time stuck between the same four walls for weeks on end. Sure, she gardened, went to the grocery store and church, but he wasn't sure she ever really spent time with friends. And since he'd left home all those years ago, he wasn't even sure she had many of those.

He really should ask, really should know more about his mom's life than he did. Especially since he wanted her to upend her entire life and move here.

Pretty fucking high-handed of you, isn't it?

Yep.

Shit.

The door opened at that moment and Gabby smiled up at him, driving out all the other thoughts in his head except one. This was where he was supposed to be right now.

"Hi."

"Hey."

They spoke in perfect unison, which he hoped was a sign of better things to come.

And when her smile widened, instinct took over.

Reaching for her, he wrapped his hands around her waist and lifted her until her feet were off the floor and her lips were level with his. Her eyes widened but her arms had already slid around his neck and she met him halfway.

Their lips met in a rush of heat that felt like a bomb detonated in his gut. Adrenaline crashed through his veins, sending sparks through his nervous system. Need swamped him, threatening his control as she opened her mouth and kissed him hard and deep.

Her taste flowed over his tongue as her hand slid into his hair and tugged, hard enough for his cock to stiffen into an iron rod in his jeans. Moving one hand to her ass, he urged her to wrap her legs around his waist and splayed his other hand across her back to press her even closer.

Her breasts flattened against his chest, the heat of her body seeping through the thin cotton of her shirt. Her weight barely registered as he spun around so he could press her back against the door and angle her body so he could grind his cock against her mound.

She moaned into his mouth, clutching at his shoulders, legs tightening around his waist. The form-fitting leggings she wore were warm against his palms. But he knew her skin would be even hotter against his.

Forcing himself not to overwhelm her all at once, he took the intensity of the kiss down a notch and finally, after a few more long seconds, allowed them both to come up for air.

Her smile and bright eyes made him want to rethink his plan for taking this slow.

"Nice to see you, too."

"Sorry." Not really, but... "How was your day?"

"Okay. Better now."

"How much better can I make it?"

GABBY'S SMILE widened and she squirmed a little closer. She'd been restless all day, and when Tim had finally knocked on her door, she'd known why.

Because of Tim. Because she'd known she was going to see him tonight and she couldn't stop thinking about him.

She'd managed to concentrate enough to get through work and not make a mess of things but now... Tim was a huge, hot wall of hard muscle and sleek flesh and the faster she could get her hands on him, the sooner he'd be naked and in her bed.

"You could make it great if you kiss me again."

When he did, she swore little sparks ignited under skin, making her body tingle from head to toe. And every place in between.

When he pulled away the next time, she sighed, feeling happy for the first time today. She should probably be a little worried about that, but right now...

"You wanna sit down?"

Tim appeared to consider his options, but the look in his eyes clued her in to his ultimate goal.

"Not really."

"Are you going to get tired of standing here holding me?"

"No."

"What about if I offer to give you a tour?"

"Only if it includes the bedroom."

"You've got a one-track mind."

"My mind's got a lot of tracks but right now, they all lead to the same place. Your bed."

Grinning, she rubbed the tip of her nose against his and ran her hands down his back.

"Well, you've already seen the kitchen and the living room so there's really only the bedroom left to check out."

"Good to know we're on the same wavelength."

Hitching her closer, he turned and started walking. She figured he was a smart guy. He could figure out where her bedroom was. She focused, instead, on putting her mouth on his skin, wherever it was exposed. The first three buttons on his flannel shirt were undone so she started there.

His breath hitched but his stride never faltered. Except...

"Are you limping?"

"Tweaked something in my side today—"

"Oh my god, put me down right now."

He stopped and looked down at her, eyebrows arched. "You're joking, right?"

"No, I'm not. Put me down. Now."

He did, but only after he gave her another look. "You do know I played two months with a broken toe and a bruised tibia last season."

"No, I didn't." She smacked her hand against his rock-hard abs. "And it wouldn't matter. I am not going to be the reason you throw out your back and can't play."

"Okay, then I'll just lie there and you can be on top."

Taking Tim by the hand, she grinned and led him to her room. "I think I can work with that."

⁂

"HOW DID I not know you had a cat?"

Gabby laughed as Tim and Princess stared at each other. Tim was propped up against the headboard and Princess sat at the bottom of the bed, staring at him like she wanted to eat him.

She had no idea where Princess had been hiding the other times Tim had been here, but obviously her finicky pet had figured Tim must be okay.

"Princess must have decided she likes you, otherwise you probably never would've known."

"She's huge. And is she missing part of her ear?"

"Yes and yes. She's a warrior princess."

"Looks like she's been living the good life lately."

"Are you calling my cat fat?"

Tim chuckled. "I wouldn't dare. Besides, I think Princess might eat my face. Hey, if I ask you to check in on my mom and sister this week while I'm gone, is that overstepping? This three-game road trip comes at a bad time."

"Of course. But..."

"But what?"

"Have you told them about us?"

"No." He paused. "Do you want me to?"

"Do you want them to know?"

"I guess it depends on you. Are we supposed to pretend that we're not sleeping together? You know that's not gonna work, right? I can't look at you and not want you, Gabby. Anybody who knows me is gonna figure out what's going on."

"I know. It's just...this whole thing is complicated."

"Yeah, but we knew that going in." Propping himself onto his elbow, he gazed down at her, eyes glued to hers. "And I think the word you're looking for is relationship."

"Is that what this is?"

"What word would you use?"

That was the problem. She didn't know.

"Gabby? Do we have a problem?"

"No. We don't have a problem. This isn't a problem."

"Then why do you have that look on your face?"

Instead of answering the question, she let her gaze slip to his naked chest. She could still see the marks her nails had made on his pecs as she'd dug them into his skin as she came around his cock.

And even though she was still trying to catch her breath, just being this close to him made her chest tight and her thighs clench. She wanted him to put his hand between her legs and stroke her clit until she came. Wanted him to press his thick fingers inside her and stroke that spot that made her shudder. She wanted him to slide his thigh against her aching clit before he spread her legs with his and thrust inside her again.

"Jesus, the look in your eyes." His voice held a sexy rasp. "I don't care what you call this thing between us. I don't care who you tell. Because the next time we're out in public, everyone's gonna know because I will not be able to pretend not to want you."

Good. She wanted everyone to know this man wanted her. Wanted him to think about nothing but her, to concentrate on making her lose control. Because for a few seconds, she'd felt her walls try to rebuild, brick by brick. It was self-defense, automatic. The breakup with Rich had her second-guessing every move she made.

"What if I asked you to give me some time? To give us some time to figure out our relationship without everyone watching?"

His eyes narrowed and he stilled, reminding her of a big cat stalking its prey. She never thought she'd enjoy being hunted. Guess you just needed the right man with the right look in his eyes.

"I'd say okay because I want you. I want this."

She didn't have to ask what he meant. She knew.

He wants me.

"I want this too. I want you so badly sometimes I can't breathe because every cell in my body wants me to wrap myself around you. Is that what you want to hear? Because it's all I've been thinking about for the past week. But you already know that, don't you?"

"I don't like to guess. Just be honest with me. And yourself."

"Honestly, I'm not sure I'm ready to go public."

"Because you work for the Colonials? Or because of something else?"

"There are just so many ways this can go sideways because we work for the same club."

"You want to keep this private? Fine. We're adults. We can have a relationship and no one else needs to know the first damn thing about it. Is that what you want?"

Did she? Did they never go out? Did they hide their relationship from everyone? "It's just...we work together."

"No, we don't. You work for the company who employees me. Don't make this a problem."

That one made her back stiffen. It was already a problem. Couldn't he see that?

"Shit." Tim's softly spoken curse ripped through the air like a blade. "Goddamn it. I'm sorry. That was uncalled for."

"No, it wasn't. And you're not wrong. Do you want to know why I said yes to dating Rich?"

His brows arched, surprise clearly written on his expression. "Do I? Is it going to make me want to punch him more than I already do?"

She couldn't help it. Her heart did a little jig at the thought that he wanted to go after Richard on her behalf.

"Because I couldn't have who I really wanted."

A little muscle in his jaw started to tic and she lifted her hands to run her thumb along it. "And who was that?"

"You're a smart guy." Her voice held an edge she couldn't restrain. "Figure it out."

"I already have. I just wanted to make sure you did."

He bent to kiss her, sealing his mouth over hers and chasing every rational thought out of her head except thoughts of him.

ELEVEN

"Hey, I'm home. Mom? Sunny? You here?"

Closing the door behind him, Tim dropped his bag and turned toward the living room.

The road trip had been a mixed bag of wins and losses for the team and for him. He'd come in to save one game, lost his start in a game that could've gone either way, and watched from the bench as the team battled back against a three-goal deficit to win two points against the hottest team in the central division.

He wanted to get some food, take a nap, spend some time with his family then visit Gabby. She'd been on his mind every moment he hadn't spent thinking about hockey.

Expecting to see his sister and mom sitting together on the couch, watching TV, he wasn't prepared for the gut-punch waiting for him as he watched his father rise from a chair at the dining room table to face him.

Blood rushed to Tim's head in a lava flow of anger.

"What the hell are you doing here? Where's Mom and Sunny?"

His father's expression remained a calm mask of civility.

"Hello, Tim. I'd ask how you're doing, but apparently nothing has changed since the last time we spoke."

Tim's anger made it almost impossible for him to speak, but he took a couple of deep breaths to try to contain it. "Since that was almost three years ago, you'd be wrong. Where are Mom and Sunny?"

His dad's chin tipped up, his gaze direct. "They went out to get something for dinner." He paused, as if he knew his next statement was going to piss Tim off. "And to give us time to talk."

Tim crossed his arms over his chest before he realized it was a classic defensive posture. *Fuck it.* "I don't have anything to say to you."

"You've made that pretty clear for the past three years. But I have something to say to you."

"I'm pretty sure I don't want to hear it."

His father showed the first signs of frustration, which was amazing because his father's usual state was frustration.

"Well, that's too bad, because you're going to listen. Because it's what your mother wants."

"Mom knows how I feel about you. She wouldn't force me to talk to you—"

"Obviously, you don't know your mother that well, because she's the one who asked me to come. I'm starting a new job in New York tomorrow morning."

"You must want something. When do you ever take into account what Mom wants?"

Tim saw his dad's temper rise in the color of his cheeks. But instead of flying off the handle like he normally would, he held his tongue. Which was more than Tim could say for himself.

"Yeah, I want something. I want to see my wife before I take a three-month job halfway across the country from her."

It was on the tip of Tim's tongue to ask if he wanted to see his daughter, too. Or was she just an afterthought. But his dad continued before he could.

"And since both of my children are in the same place at the same time, I thought I could say hello. But since you're loaded for bear, I guess I can forget that."

Tim opened his mouth to fire back at his dad, but some safety switch clicked on before the words escaped. It'd been years since he'd seen his dad, years where he'd tried to put the fighting and the misery and the anger behind him.

He couldn't remember a time when they weren't fighting. It was just what they did. And not even a minute after he and his dad were in the same room, even after three years apart, they were at each other's throats.

And that was his fault, Tim realized. His dad hadn't started this. He had.

Goddammit.

Old habits were so fucking hard to break.

He didn't want to be this guy for Gabby. He wanted to be better.

Looking his father in the eyes, he took a deep breath. "Sorry. Shouldn't have jumped down your throat."

Then he swallowed down every bit of anger he could manage. There was still enough to choke a horse, but he kept silently repeating Gabby's name. He was better than this, damn it. He could be the better man.

His father couldn't hide his shock, which gave Tim a guilty thrill. But hey, he wasn't perfect.

"You want a beer?"

Tim thought his dad might actually say no just to spite him.

"Sure. Thanks."

Tim headed for the kitchen, heard his dad following along behind.

"Nice place."

Christ, here it comes. Tim wondered if this was about the money he'd been sending his mom. Or maybe he was here to ask for money.

"You've done well for yourself."

Tim grabbed a couple of beers from the fridge, not knowing or caring if his dad would even like what he grabbed. Didn't matter. His dad would drink it or not.

"I've done okay."

"Turned thirty-one this past year. You decided how long you're going to play?"

Was his dad deliberately trying to piss him off? He couldn't tell.

Just breathe. He won't be here forever.

"No."

"Caught some of the game on TV last night."

Tim couldn't hide his surprise and his dad saw it right away. His mouth twisted in grimace Tim remembered well from his childhood.

"You held up well even though the team played shaky in front of you."

Well, damn. Look at that. He and his dad actually agreed on something.

"Not our best game."

"No, it wasn't."

Tim took a long pull on his beer as an uncomfortable silence fell between them.

Finally, his dad sighed and shook his head. "I know you've been trying to get your mom to move out here with you."

Shit. Was he really going to go there? Before Tim could answer, his dad continued.

"Do you know why she won't?"

Was that a trick question? How the hell was he supposed to answer that? Did he really expect an answer?

"Because she loves me. And she knows I love her."

Tim's mouth dropped open in shock at his dad's declaration. Just the simple fact that Craig Stanton had used the word "love" in connection with his wife was enough to send Tim's head reeling.

Then his dad continued like he hadn't turned Tim's world upside down.

"If you get married, you'll understand that things aren't always perfect between two people. You and I, we're never going to see eye to eye. But for the sake of your mother, let's not make this a pissing contest. If you keep pushing her to leave me, you may get what you want. But it won't be for the reasons you want."

Well, hell. What did he say to that?

"And while you're speechless, let me say something else. You made something of yourself and you make me proud."

Tim finally remembered to close his mouth. Never in a million years had he expected his dad to say anything like the words that just came out of his mouth. Tim had no idea how to respond. Couldn't think of a damn thing to say.

His dad nodded. "Now, your mom and Sunny'll be back soon. Said they were going to get pizza, but they'll probably come back with some gourmet shit. I'll watch a game while you put your stuff away. And I'll take another beer."

"AND THEN HE ate dinner and left?"

"Yeah. I felt like I was in the fucking Twilight Zone."

"Any idea what made him do that?"

"No clue. I don't know if my mom said something to him or Sunny. Hell, maybe he's dying and he's doing a farewell tour." He paused. "*Shit.* I don't want him to die. You know that, right?"

Tim shifted on the bed so he could look down at Gabby. She'd turned her naked body into his and laid her head on his chest. They'd been lying here for the past half hour, catching their breath after tearing each other's clothes off seconds after he'd knocked on her door late Tuesday night. They'd had a date for dinner last night, but his dad's surprise visit had thrown off their plans. He hadn't felt right leaving his apartment while his entire family was there.

He'd spent tonight's game on the bench, watching Shane get his mojo back. The younger guy had been struggling and Tim had seen a few TV talking heads recently wondering if the Colonials were going to call up DeAngelo from Reading or "see if they could count on Stanton to start pulling his weight."

It was a legitimate question, one only Tim could answer. And right now, he had no fucking clue what the answer should be.

"I know you don't." Her voice sounded lazy, a little sleepy, a little amused. "Was your mom happy to see him?"

"I guess. I don't know. I love my mom, but I'm starting to think she's never going to be truly happy."

Gabby lifted her head and propped her chin on her balled fist on his chest. "Why do you say that?"

"Because nothing seems to make her happy. Maybe this is how she's always been, and I just never noticed it. Or maybe she just thinks I'm too much like my dad."

"Do you think you're too much like your dad?"

He shook his head immediately. "But I realized last night, I'm a lot more like him than I thought."

"You're not your dad, Tim. And you're not going to turn into him, either."

"I want to believe that." Tim sighed. "Sometimes, though, I'll say something, and I swear I sound just like him. And we're both stubborn as hell."

"Stubborn isn't always a bad thing.

"Unless you're using it against me."

Her smile lit up his world. He wondered if she knew that. He'd do whatever it took to keep her smiling at him like that.

"I'll keep that in mind." She batted her eyes at him, but the innocent look she gave him made him laugh. "And I'm not the only one with a stubborn streak, you know."

"That look gets you whatever you want from your dad, doesn't it?"

"Of course. And it doesn't work on you?"

"You know it does." And he was okay with that.

"Good. Wouldn't want to think I was losing my touch."

"Speaking of touch..."

He ran his hand up her naked back, her skin warm against his, the look in her eyes getting even warmer when he ran his hand back down her spine to the curve of her ass.

She made a soft, purring sound as he petted her ass and she stretched next to him like a cat.

"Don't forget, you have to be up early tomorrow to catch the bus for the DC game."

"You want me to stop?"

Flipping her over onto her back, he spread out on top of her, nestling his cock between her thighs. She sucked in a quick, harsh breath before smoothing her hands down his back to his ass.

"You can sleep on the bus."

Then she kissed him and they didn't sleep at all for the next hour.

"HEY, MAN. EVERYTHING OKAY?"

RJ slid into the seat across from Tim ten minutes after the

buses left the parking lot Wednesday headed for DC. The team would stay overnight tonight, play a rare, weekday five p.m. game tomorrow then bus back home tomorrow night.

"Yeah. I'm fine. Why?"

RJ shrugged. "You've been quiet. Didn't know if something was going on."

Yeah. Actually, there was a hell of a lot going on. But he could only tell RJ some of it. Which was part of the reason Tim had been quiet. And it sucked.

He should tell RJ he was fine, but he didn't want to lie. He was already doing enough of that. Since Gabby still wanted to keep their relationship under wraps, Tim couldn't tell his best friend, her brother, how frustrated he was. He couldn't talk to his mom about it for the same reason, and if he told his sister, he wasn't sure she'd be able to keep her mouth shut. Not out of spite, but because she'd be happy for him.

"I'm fine." Then he grimaced and shrugged a shoulder. "Had a visit from my dad Monday."

RJ's eyes went wide. "Whoa. Seriously? I didn't know you were talking."

"We did Monday. He stopped at my place on his way to New York for a job. We didn't come to blows so I'd call it a success."

"Damn. Why didn't you say anything yesterday?"

Tim arched his brows. "We had a game yesterday."

RJ's grimace looked painful. "Yeah. That kinda sucked, didn't it?"

"I should ask how you're holding up."

"Fine." When Tim just continued to stare at him, RJ held up a hand. "No, seriously. I mean, yeah, it sucked playing against my old team, but after all the shit that went down last season, what some of the guys said about me, I don't miss them. I'm glad to be here."

"And we're glad to have you."

"So, you wanna come over and get stupid drunk Sunday after the game?"

They had a one p.m. game Sunday. He'd planned to spend at least part of the night with Gabby, but RJ sounded like he could use a friend. He could always go over to her place afterward.

He wanted to take her to the benefit as his date. Not just meet her there and pretend to be friends who just happened to be at the same event.

"Yeah, sounds like a plan."

A slight pause before RJ leaned back and studied him.

"What?"

"Something else going on?"

The words sat on his tongue. He wanted to talk about Gabby, wanted RJ's advice on how to handle the situation. And he knew if he told RJ not to say anything, he wouldn't. But that just meant Tim broke his word to Gabby.

"No. Everything's fine."

Maybe if he said it enough, it'd be true.

"HEY, Mom, you know I pay a cleaning service, right? You don't have to clean my kitchen."

"I don't want them to think you're a slob, Timmy. And I'm just wiping things down."

Which was why she had all the cleaning products he owned sitting on the counter while she leaned into the corner with a rag in her hand Friday morning. He'd come in to grab something for breakfast before heading to the arena for practice with the team.

"Can you let that go for a minute? I need to talk. Where's Sunny?"

"She said she was going to the market. Did you sleep okay?"

"You let her go alone? Does she even know where she's going?"

Now, his mom stopped and gave him her full attention. And a piece of her mind. Shit, what the hell had he said?

"Your sister's more than competent enough to navigate a big city on her own. She's an adult. You do know that, right?"

"Yeah, I just..." He sighed. "Sorry. I've got a lot on my mind and... That was stupid."

"Just a little," his mom agreed with a nod. "So what's on your mind? Are you still upset about your dad's visit? I know we shouldn't have sprung that on you, but your dad promised there'd be no fighting and you two are more than old enough to get along civilly."

"I told you, I'm not mad about that. Actually, this doesn't have anything to do with that."

"Is something wrong? Are you hurt?"

"No, not hurt." He sat on one of the stools at the island while she leaned on the other side, cleaning rag abandoned for now. "I'm thinking about retiring after this season."

She didn't say anything for several seconds, probably in shock.

Then she nodded. "Okay. Do you know what you want to do next?"

Well, shit. He was the one who was shocked.

"That's it? Just...okay?"

"Why do you seem so surprised?" His mom's rare smile appeared. "After your birthday last year, I knew you'd started thinking about it."

"How? Did I say something? Do something?"

"No, nothing that really stood out." Then she shrugged. "You're my son. I know you. So, have you made plans?"

"I have a couple ideas."

"What does Gabby think about this?"

He paused, his brain spinning. "Why would Gabby care?"

She gave him the mom look. "Please. I know she's the girl you've been seeing. And I see the way you look at her. Is there a reason you don't want people to know you're dating? Because she's the general manager's daughter?"

Looked like that cat was out of the bag. "I don't care who knows. Gabby's the one who wants us to keep it under wraps. She thinks it'll look bad if she's dating a player."

"Hmm. Well, I can see her point. Has to be hard for her to be the daughter of the GM and the sister of two players. And then to be dating a player, too? Tough position."

"I guess. Yeah."

"Is she part of the reason you're thinking about retiring? Because if you're doing it for anyone other than yourself—"

"No. I'm not retiring just so I can date her. I just...think it's time. I'm not getting any younger, my body's starting to wear down, and I don't want to be in the position where I get injured and have to make a decision on the spot. But I don't know if I'm giving up too soon."

"Only you can know that. But don't doubt yourself, sweetheart. You've come so far, farther than so many people get in life, because you listened to yourself. You trusted yourself. Why would you stop now?"

"Maybe because there's a lot more at stake and I'm worried..."

"Worried about what?"

"That I'm doing this for the wrong reasons."

"And what would be a wrong reason?"

He didn't answer right away but his mom apparently knew him better than he realized.

"That you're doing it for her?" She raised her brows at him. "Why would that be wrong?"

"Maybe because I don't have a clue what's going to happen. I don't know what the hell I'm going to do with my life. I mean, I have some ideas, but I don't know if I'll be able to make them happen. And what if Gabby and I don't work out?"

"Nothing comes with a guarantee. Hell, even guarantees aren't for certain. There's always a loophole somewhere. But honey, what if you don't take the chance and you wind up bitter, old, and alone? That would be even worse."

It was an opening to ask a question he'd been dying to ask his mom for years but had never found the right moment.

"Is that why you stay with him? So you won't be alone?"

He thought for a few seconds that she wouldn't answer. Finally, she drew in a deep breath.

"I know you're going to find it hard to believe, but I love your father. We've had our moments, when I considered leaving him. Most of those times had to do with you." She held up one hand to halt his words. "You and he are just never going to get along. And he knows it's his fault. He knows your relationship is permanently damaged because he wasn't the man you needed him to be. But he's not that man with me. Do you understand?"

"Yeah, I think so. I'm not ready to be his BFF but I don't hate him."

"Then there's hope. Now, what are you going to do about Gabby?"

He shook his head. "I'm going to hope she's willing to take me as I am. Now, I've got a phone call to make. And Mom...thanks."

"TIM, are you really sure this is what you want to do? You don't have to make up your mind immediately. The season's only half over. You could change your mind in a couple of weeks."

Doug Mitchell stared across his desk, his shock slowly fading at Tim's declaration that this would be his last season.

"I've given it a lot of thought and I've decided this is what I need to do. For myself."

Mitchell took a breath, leaning back into his chair. His eyebrows slowly lowered back to their normal position as he shook his head.

"I don't get involved in players' lives. It's not my place. But Tank... you're having a good year. Sure, there've been a few rough patches, but everyone has those. I get the idea about wanting to go out on top. It's completely valid. When I retired, my coach tried to talk me out of it. Told me I had at least another three good years. But I knew it was the best thing for me at the time. And for my family. I was on the verge of being traded, and I didn't want to uproot my family again. Those last couple of years were tough. We moved three times in six years. My kids didn't deserve to go through that again. So I get it. And I'll support whatever you decide. It's a big decision."

"I'm aware this might seem like it's coming out of left field, but it's not." After talking to his mom, he knew it was the right decision. "It's something I've been thinking about for the past year. And it's not something I'm taking lightly."

"I'm sure you're not. And I'm not trying to talk you out of it. I just want you to be sure." He paused but Tim knew he wasn't finished. He was considering his words carefully. "Now, you can tell me to keep my opinions to myself, but I think you've got another couple of years in you. That's speaking as a general manager who's gonna be really sorry to lose the best backup in the league."

The praise was unexpected and humbling. And he nodded to acknowledge.

"But if you're going to do this, I hope you have a plan." Tim opened his mouth, but before he got a word out, Mitchell continued. "And if you don't, I'd like you to hear me out."

TWELVE

"Rich. I wasn't expecting you. What are you doing here?"

"Hello, Gabrielle. I'm here to do you a favor."

She blinked, momentarily dumbfounded. "A favor. I didn't know I needed one."

"I believe you'll thank me when you hear what I have to say."

Gabby's smile felt more like a grimace as she stared at her former lover. A man she couldn't honestly believe she'd ever wanted to spend time with, much less have sex with. Now, she saw him for what he truly was.

A petty asshole.

She wanted him gone as soon as possible. And she really didn't want to invite him into her office, especially not at four o'clock on a Friday afternoon when everyone else had already left for the day.

She was literally the only person on this floor, everyone having left early because of the home game tomorrow night. The team had had practice earlier so most of them were gone as well, off to enjoy a rare free Friday. She'd planned to see Tim tonight, had hoped he'd call. They'd talked every night since

Monday, the last time they'd seen each other. But there'd been something in Tim's voice, something...off.

She'd almost walked down to the ice, just to catch a glimpse of him, but she'd told herself it would look suspicious. Especially if she stood there and blatantly watched Tim practice.

And now she had to deal with Rich. *Ugh.*

"Okay." She hoped her voice didn't sound as unwelcoming as she thought it did. "I guess you should come in."

She walked back to her desk; putting it between them made her feel a little better. "What can I help you with?"

He stopped directly in front of it, his smug expression making her want to bare her teeth. "I thought you'd want to know RJ's case is going to get more complicated this week."

Her stomach dropped and she was pretty sure all the blood in her head rushed to her feet. Swallowing hard, she straightened her spine and gave him her best "you're an asshole" smile. "How so?"

Reaching into his coat pocket, he withdrew an envelope and tossed it onto her desk. For some reason, the action felt like a threat.

Now you're just overreacting. Chill.

"I was told these pictures were on their way to a television station in L.A. I thought you should have a heads up."

Photos. Of RJ. He had photos of her brother. She reached for the envelope, trying not to treat it like a bomb about to explode in her face. Spilling them out into her hand, she leafed through them. By the time she was done, her temples throbbed with stress and anger.

They were definitely of RJ. Couldn't deny that. His face showed plainly in every photo. And they'd obviously been taken at a party. Was it the same party where he'd been accused, along with several other former teammates, of assaulting two women?

The woman in the photo might have been one of the women

accusing him. She certainly looked like the blonde who'd been all over the news, the twenty-one-year-old who managed to look sixteen.

Shit. Shit. Shit.

"I was sure you'd want to see them before they made it onto the air. RJ doesn't exactly look not-guilty in those. I know you've been worried. Maybe I can help you with this situation."

Bastard. He sounded actually happy about it.

"And how exactly did you get these?"

"A friend of a friend with connections in L.A. I thought, if you'd calmed down since your snit a few weeks ago, maybe I could give you a hand. Maybe discuss this over dinner tonight."

She caught her mouth from dropping open but only barely.

Calmed down. Snit. Dinner.

"That's not going to happen."

His expression didn't change and that was creepier than anything else he could have done. "I think you're making a mistake. Why don't you take a little time to think about my offer?"

"Your offer of dinner or your offer for me to go to dinner with you in exchange for your silence about these pictures? I need you to spell out what you're saying right now. Are you threatening to release this information if I don't go out with you?"

He looked like she'd made a lewd comment and he was someone's really ugly spinster aunt. "Of course not. Like I said, you misunderstood. I'm trying to do you a favor. I wanted you to know what I'd heard. That's all. I'm not threatening you. That's absurd. Why would I do that?"

Gabby could think of one damn good reason why he would. Because she'd broken up with him. And women didn't break up with Rich. He dumped them.

She wanted to say that out loud and watch him try to talk it away. Or gaslight her into believing she was the one at fault. But this bastard had threatened her brother and, until she figured out exactly what game he was playing, she couldn't do it.

"It certainly sounded like a threat to me."

Gabby turned toward the man who'd spoken. Tim stood in the doorway, anger plainly visible on his face. Obviously, he'd listened to their conversation long enough to figure out what was going on. And he was about to make things very much worse.

"Are you okay, Gabby?"

"I'm fine. Tim—"

"Do you always walk into an office when the door's closed?" Rich's smirk set Gabby's teeth on edge. "This is a private conversation."

"Not when you're trying to blackmail a woman into going out with you." Tim's face was set in granite lines. "What kind of sick fuck does that?"

Shit.

A flush suffused Rich's face. "That's not what's going on here, but I wouldn't expect you to understand that."

She needed to get a handle on this. Now. "Tim—"

"I understand a hell of a lot more than you think I do, asshole." Tim took a few steps closer. "She said she wasn't going out with you. Take the hint. Leave the photos and if I see them on ESPN or the NHL Network, I'm gonna know who they came from and I'm going to kick your ass."

Gabby wanted to roll her eyes at the testosterone flying around the room right now. She couldn't say she was sorry Tim had walked in when he did, but now he was making a mess of a situation she didn't want him anywhere near.

"Tim, no." She put her hand on his arm, his bicep tight and hard as rock beneath her palm. "He's not worth your career."

"What career? He's a second-rate backup whose time has

passed." Richard laughed, an ugly sound she barely heard because her entire attention had switched to Tim. "You'll be traded before the year's out. You'll be lucky to play in the AHL next season."

"I think it's time for you to go, Rich." The words practically stuck in her throat, but she forced them out. "Thanks for the heads-up."

"I'm sure I'll be hearing from you, Gabby. Have a good night."

She could practically hear Tim's teeth grind, but he didn't make a move toward the door as Rich slithered away.

A gut-wrenching anger churned in her stomach, most of it directed at Rich, that bastard. But a tiny part of it was focused on the man glaring down at her. She knew it wasn't fair, knew it wasn't even rational. But she couldn't help herself.

"Why the hell didn't you call me when he showed up? He's dangerous, Gabby."

And when he spoke down to her like she was a child, she wanted to turn and walk out on him. But it was her office, goddammit.

"I had the situation under control until you got here. Then you two started a pissing contest."

"He was fucking blackmailing you."

"Were you listening at the door?"

"The door was partially closed, and I heard voices. So yeah, I listened to make sure I wasn't interrupting anything." He paused. "Wait. Are you *mad* at me? Seriously?"

"I was handling him." It was damn hard to speak through her gritted teeth. "You can't just walk in here like you own me—"

"What the hell? I don't think I own you. I was *worried* about you. What if he'd done more than just threaten you? That guy's got serious issues."

"Do you think I don't know that? That I'm not smart enough to figure that out? *I* dumped *him*, remember? I don't need a caretaker. I don't need another father."

"Then what do you need?"

"I need someone who believes that I can take care of myself. Who doesn't treat me like a child who needs protection."

"There's a difference between wanting to protect someone you love and treating an adult like a child."

She blinked. Had he just—

"Yeah, I said it." He stared her down, his expression softening only slightly. "I mean it. I don't care who knows. I love you. I have for years. I'm still not sure why our relationship has to be a goddamn state secret."

How could he not understand, after what had just happened, why she'd want to keep their affair out of the limelight?

"Tim—"

She cut off when he held up a hand, shaking his head and looking away.

"No, just listen for a second." He took a deep breath. "I'm sorry you think I'm treating you like a child. I don't see it that way. My first instinct is to keep you safe. My first thought is for you."

Her heart melted, but he continued before she could say anything.

"But I don't want to be the secret you keep hidden from everyone." He stopped, took a deep breath, and shook his head. "You have to be willing to meet me halfway. I want you and I'm not afraid for people to know. I'm gonna go. I think we can both use some space."

She bit her tongue against the need to say whatever it took to make him stay. Because he was right. She needed time to process.

She wanted to say something, anything. But she didn't even know where to start.

"I'll make sure that asshole's gone." Tim spoke over his shoulder as he headed for the door. "Call me if he hassles you again. Talk to you soon."

He walked through the door, leaving her blinking at his retreating back.

"HEY, I need to talk to you about something."

RJ lowered the volume on the west-coast game he and Tim were half-heartedly watching Sunday night. Sitting in RJ's living room, they both had ice packs on various parts of their body—RJ's shoulder and Tim's thigh—and were drinking beer, ignoring the fact they'd both played shitty games this weekend.

RJ hadn't said anything about the pictures that asshole had given Gabby, so he didn't know if RJ just didn't want to talk about it or if Gabby hadn't said anything to him. He was betting on the latter. She probably wanted to have a plan in place before she told RJ. He understood her motivation, but it was RJ's life being fucked with. The guy deserved to know. But if Tim told him, Gabby would know where RJ had found out. She'd be pissed and he figured she was already angry enough with him.

"Yeah, sure. What's up?"

"Talked to your dad yesterday. Told him I was retiring at the end of the season."

"Holy shit. Seriously?" RJ looked surprised but not shocked. "I mean, I know you said you were thinking about it, but it seems kinda fast. What'd Dad say?"

"Tried to talk me out of it at first. Then he gave me something to think about."

"Did he change your mind?"

"Not about quitting, no. But he did float an idea. He asked if I'd thought about becoming a goalie coach."

RJ's brows drew down. "Really? Is Ellis retiring? No, wait. Collins. In Reading. I heard he was having some health issues."

"Yeah, I heard that too, but your dad didn't say and I didn't ask."

"So what'd you tell him?"

"That I'd think about it."

"And are you?"

"Yeah. I am."

RJ shook his head. "Damn, you're really going to go through with it? You're gonna retire? Did something happen? Or is there something else going on? Like maybe something with my sister?"

Tim paused long enough for RJ's lips to curve in a shit-eating grin. "And if I said yes?"

"I'd say I don't need details but good luck."

The humor in RJ's voice made Tim smile but it was fleeting. "It's complicated."

"Yeah, no shit." RJ snorted. "Gabby's complicated. I mean, she's my sister and I love her but she's so damn practical, I just wanna shake her. I'm not sure she ever has any fun." He paused. "And I absolutely do not ever want to know what kind of fun you guys have. Man, I wanna be a good friend, but this is testing my limits."

Tim laughed, leaning over and clinking his bottle against RJ's. "Don't worry. There's no way in hell I'm discussing my sex life with you."

RJ winced. "Aw, man, do you even have to say that word in relation to my sister? Not cool."

"I love her."

"Eh. Yeah, kinda knew that."

Hell, maybe everyone who knew him did.

"I'm not sure she loves me. Something happened Thursday...and we haven't talked since. I'm not sure anything I said would help right now."

"Did you have a fight? She can get pretty stubborn when she wants to be. She's not mean about it. She's just..."

"Immoveable."

"Yeah, kinda like someone else I know."

RJ gave him a look. Tim gave him the finger.

"I don't know what I'm going to do. Not sure what I can do because there're other issues—"

"Issues like what? Like she's my sister and you're my best friend?"

"That's part of it, yeah. There's other shit too."

"Shit I should know about?"

"Probably, yeah. Fuck it. She's gonna know where you heard this, but you need to hear."

By the time he'd told RJ about the situation with Rich and the pictures, Tim felt like a fucking tattletale. And a really fucking bad friend. RJ had gone sheet white before his cheeks had bloomed fire-engine red.

"Why the fuck didn't she tell me?"

"Because she figures you have enough on your plate, and she wanted to take care of it before it affected you. I'm pretty sure she would've handled it and then told you about it. Your sister likes to have everything in its box. I think she's forgotten that not everything fits in a box. Sometimes life's messy."

"Did you see the pictures?"

"Yeah. It's nothing graphic, but I'm pretty sure it shows you with your arms around one of the women who's suing you."

"And that asshole she used to date had them?"

"Yeah. But if he goes after you or Gabby, I'm pretty sure he knows I'm going to beat him into next week. And then I'll make sure to tell the world what an asshole he is."

"So basically you stuck up for her and she thought you were trying to control her life. Yep. Sounds like Gabby. She's the only one allowed to deal with this shit. Christ, what a fucking mess."

When RJ started to swear, Tim knew his mood had taken a nosedive. "What are you gonna do?"

RJ shook his head, eyes closed. "I gotta talk to Gabby. I'm so sorry, man. She's gonna know you told me."

"I know."

"When are you gonna tell her about retiring?"

"No clue." Tim tipped back the rest of his beer. "I don't know when I'm gonna talk to her again. And after you talk to her, I'm not sure she's gonna want to talk to me. Again."

"She will. She's stubborn. Not stupid."

"But I'm not sure she loves me."

"She'd be stupid not to."

"GABBY, you can't keep shit like this from me. When were you gonna tell me?"

"After I'd made sure I'd taken care of it. You have enough to worry about. And this is my job. I can't believe Tim tol—"

"No." Tim sliced a hand out in front of him. "You don't get to take this out on Tim. He's not the one at fault. You should've come to me right away. I know you wanted to take care of it. But it's not your job to keep things like this away from me, especially when they affect my life. I have to know what's coming at me."

Damn it. *Damn it.* She hated being wrong.

"You're right. I'm sorry."

"I'm not the only one you need to tell you're sorry."

She winced, guilty and angry and hurt and not knowing how to get past it.

RJ had knocked on her office door Tuesday morning,

looking like a cover model in his suit and tie. The team's last game before the holiday break was tonight and her brain buzzed with so many details about that and the upcoming holiday

She'd been surprised to see him this early but then she'd looked at her watch and realized it was close to noon. She'd been keeping herself busy, her brain filled with last-minute details for the team and the holidays. Trying not to think about Tim.

Which was exactly what RJ wanted her to think about.

She looked him straight in the eyes. "I don't know what you're talking about."

RJ's brows arched. "Don't bullshit me, little sister. And don't bullshit yourself. You know he was right to tell me."

The urge to pout and stamp her feet like a child nearly overwhelmed her but, damn it again, he was right. And that just made it all worse. She'd spent the weekend moping because she wasn't with Tim. Had watched him go in to save the game Sunday only to lose it by letting in another two goals. Wondered if their fight had had anything to do with his state of mind, then wondered if she was giving herself too much credit. Except...

"I love you."

He'd said the words. And she'd stood there and stared at him like he had grown an extra head.

Sighing, she picked up a pencil from her desk and tossed it across the desk at RJ.

"Why are you not threatening to scalp me?"

RJ's half-hearted grin hurt her heart. "Because I love you and I know you thought you were doing the right thing. But this mess is mine. The mess with Tim... That's all on you."

Not caring how old she was, she made a face and stuck out her tongue.

"*That* is definitely none of your business."

RJ laughed but she could tell his heart wasn't in it. "Hey, if you can meddle in my life, I get to meddle in yours. Wanna tell me why you're keeping him at arms' length?"

She hadn't exactly kept Tim at arms' length, but she was pretty sure her brother didn't want to hear how close Tim had gotten to her.

"What if it doesn't work out? A relationship with a player can be messy but having to work together after a breakup? It would be hell."

Just thinking about it gave her heart palpitations. But just saying the word "breakup" out loud had hurt.

"And if you don't even try?" RJ shook his head. "That's worse. Word of advice? Don't think about it too long. You're both stubborn as hell. You're gonna need to bend a little."

"CAN I COME IN?"

Gabby's door was open, but Tim knocked before he stepped inside. He wasn't sure what kind of reception he was going to get, and he'd purposely only given himself enough time to spend a few minutes here. He had to be in the locker room in fifteen minutes to get ready for the game.

Sitting at her desk, Gabby looked up and smiled. A little. So far, so good.

"Of course."

She bit her lip, as if she wanted to say something else. But she must have reconsidered because she smiled and remained silent.

Okay. Guess it was up to him.

"You mind if I close the door?"

"No, go ahead."

He turned to shut it and, when he turned back, she'd stood and come around her desk to lean back against it.

She looked amazing. Her hair a sleek fall of waves that he wanted to sink his hands into, her lips a pretty shade of pink he wanted to taste, and her brown eyes staring into his with a heat he swore he could feel.

"About Friday—"

"I'm sorry." She broke in before he could finish. "I shouldn't have reacted the way I did. It was a knee-jerk reaction and I'm sorry for jumping down your throat."

"And I'm sorry for acting like a caveman and making things worse. I know you can take care of yourself. But I can't help wanting to take care of you."

Her smile widened. "And that's okay most of the time. It was just a combination of things—"

"I told your dad I'm retiring at the end of the season."

Her mouth dropped open in shock and stayed that way for several seconds before she snapped it shut and blinked in shock.

"What?"

"I told you I was thinking about it. I made up my mind. I'm ready to move on."

Did her cheeks go a little pale? Was she happy? Sad? What?

"I don't want you to think I'm doing this because of you. I'm doing this for myself. And because I want us to give a relationship a shot."

She shook her head, her brow furrowing. "Do you think you need to give up your career for *me*?"

He shook his head, feeling like he was crossing thin ice. "No. I know you wouldn't ask me to do that. You barely ask me to do anything for you."

"What does that mean?"

"Nothing. It doesn't mean anything. Gabby—"

"No." She held up her hand. "Just...wait. I don't want to fight. But I also don't want to be the reason you retire."

"I'm not retiring *for* you. And I'm not retiring *because* of you."

"Tim..."

"I'm retiring because *this* is when I've decided to retire. On my terms."

Her gaze darted away for a few, telling seconds. "If that's what you truly want, then I'm happy for you. But if you think this is what I *want* you to do—"

"No. That's not it."

"Okay." She paused, her expression not loosening at all. "Do you know what you're going to do?"

"I have a couple of ideas, yeah. One that would keep me in the area. Close to you."

Her eyes widened, and he couldn't tell if he saw fear or surprise cross her expression. Whichever, it was gone in a flash.

"And that's what *you* want?"

She'd gone so still, watching his every move.

Nodding, he watched her carefully. "Yeah, it is. But you have to know if it's what you want. I don't want to push you into a relationship if you're not ready—"

"I didn't say I wasn't ready. But we literally have only been together two weeks. How do you know we'll still be together in a month? A year?"

He shrugged. "I don't. I do know I've loved you for years. I want to be with you. The question is, do you want me?"

Her lips parted and she drew in a breath, but he stood and closed the space between them before she could say something he might not want to hear.

Instead, he sealed his mouth over hers in a kiss that made him sweat. And want. Christ, he wanted her.

His mouth devoured hers, her taste an aphrodisiac that made his heart pound and his stiffening cock ruin the line of his suit. It didn't help when she lifted her arms and wrapped them around his neck, pressing the full length of her body against his. Giving him exactly what he wanted.

Christ, he'd missed this. Wanted so much more than her mouth on his. He wanted to run his hands up her back and press her even closer. Wanted to strip her clothes away until she stood naked in front of him and he would go to his knees and—

With a groan, he set her away from him, loving the fact that she gripped his shoulders tight before letting him go.

"Think about it, Gabby. Don't answer now, just think about us. I'll see you at the benefit tomorrow. Do you want me to pick you up?"

"No, I'll meet you there. I have an appointment before." She slowly released his shoulders, where she'd been gripping him tight. She looked flushed and out of breath. "Tim, I—"

"I'll see you tomorrow night."

And he hoped like hell she'd want to dance with him for more than just one night.

THIRTEEN

"Whoa, Gabby. You look amazing. Guess you're not spending the night at home watching TV."

Gabby rolled her eyes at RJ and waved him through her front door as she finished fastening her earrings.

No, she wasn't, but she'd briefly considered it. She knew if she showed up at this event tonight, she'd have to make a decision. She couldn't continue to string Tim along. It wasn't fair. To either of them.

"I'm about to head out the door for the Sunnyspace benefit. Hey, good game last night, by the way."

"Thanks. Guess I should've called. This can wait until tomorrow."

"You're here now. What's up? What do you need?"

"Nothing that can't wait."

Something in her brother's voice made her stop and look at him, really look. What she saw made her breath catch in her throat.

"What happened?"

For a few seconds, she thought he wasn't going to answer.

Then he sighed and straightened, like he was about to do something she wasn't going to like.

"I talked to Mom and Dad then I made a call to the *LA Times*. I told them we can do an interview Monday. They can ask me whatever they want. I have nothing to hide. I'm sick of acting like I do."

A mess of emotions roiled in her gut. Anger that anyone could think RJ would ever be guilty of any of the accusations being flung at him. Sadness at the hard edge in her older brother's normally cheerful voice. And the odd sense of guilt that someone she'd left him to handle this on his own.

"Why didn't you ask me to make that call? Or at least be there for...moral support?"

The curve of his lips held no amusement at all. "Because I'm an adult who should be able to handle his own mess." Then a hint of the normal RJ peeked out in an easier grin. "I'll have you there for the call, if that makes you feel any better."

She smiled back at him. "It does. I'm here for you. You know that, right?"

He nodded. "I know. So. All this is for Tank, huh? Glad to see you're making an effort. The poor guy won't know what hit him."

She thought about her next words carefully. "I'm still not sure what I going to do. I'm afraid I'm going to mess this up. Mess us up."

Reaching for her, he squeezed her shoulder. "Don't doubt your instincts. Tell him how you really feel. Everything else will fall into place or it won't and then you'll do what you do best."

"What's that?"

"Make it happen yourself."

GABBY THOUGHT about her brother's words all the way to the venue where they were holding the benefit. Located along the Schuylkill River, the building had been a residence years ago, a mansion that'd been lovingly restored by a local historical society. Today, it held events like this one.

Stepping through the huge, arched wood doors, she was glad she'd taken the time to get her hair and makeup done. She felt much more at ease knowing she looked like she fit in wearing a designer dress and Louboutin heels. Most events she attended didn't call for her to dress in a couple thousand dollars of silk and rhinestones.

As she walked into the main hall, she recognized a billionaire tech mogul and five millionaires, all of whom nodded and smiled at her as she passed by. Any other night, she would've stopped to talk. She would've made the rounds, shook hands, made small talk, asked about families and golf games and invited them to a game in the box with her dad. All part of the job.

Tonight wasn't about the job. She smiled to acknowledge them but kept walking. She had one goal tonight.

A jazz quartet played softly in one corner, though no one was dancing yet. They'd save that for after dinner and the presentation of recognition awards, probably for the money these men and women had given to keep this place running. Men like Tim.

Anticipation rushed through her at the thought of being in his arms. She hadn't seen him after the game last night. She'd gotten caught up with a couple of chatty sponsors after the game and he'd been gone before she made it downstairs. Then she'd wondered if he'd deliberately avoided her.

Which was ridiculous. After what he'd said to her...why would he avoid her?

Maybe because he thinks you're going to dump him? You do have kind of a reputation.

Just the thought made her stomach hurt. All she'd thought about every waking hour since yesterday was Tim. And how much she wanted him to stay here. With her. The thought of him leaving the team made her heart hurt because she wouldn't be able to see him every day. And that just wasn't acceptable.

She needed to tell him that. Needed to tell him she wanted to be with him, and she didn't care who was here that would see them. In fact, she was pretty sure she wanted everyone to know he was hers. And she was his.

"May I have this dance?"

Tim spoke directly into her ear, his voice resonating deep inside her. Smiling, she turned—and had to remind herself to breathe.

The man looked like the fairytale prince she'd dreamed of as a child but had grown up to believe didn't exist. Yet, here he was, a hockey god in a tux made specifically for his body. A tux she wanted to strip away so she could get her hands on the hard body beneath.

"You cut your hair."

She took the hand he held out to her as she reached with her other to brush through the silky strands. They'd been cut short enough to only hint at the curls she knew were there.

His smile widened as she stepped into his body, pressed tight enough that she could feel the heat of him. A heat that only intensified as she came even closer.

"You look so civilized."

"And you look amazing." His voice brushed against her ear. "I'm glad you came."

"Did you think I wouldn't?"

He paused. "I might've considered it a few times."

Now or never.

"Of course, I came. I couldn't miss an opportunity to dance with you."

She hadn't realized they'd begun to sway to the music, their bodies in perfect rhythm, until Tim stopped, his hands on her hips gripping her hard before loosening.

"Gabby."

She closed the sliver of air left between their bodies and pressed her body tightly to his. She wanted to be clear about her intentions.

"I want to have dinner together and then I want to dance with you some more," she said. "I don't care who sees us or who talks about us. I don't care what anyone else thinks. I only care what you think. And if you want to leave now and go back to my place, I'd be okay with that, too."

He pulled his head back and put one hand under her chin so she couldn't look away. "I don't just want you in my bed, Gabby. I want you in my life. I want you to *be* my life."

The tightness in her chest that had plagued her all day cracked and let her take her first full breath, maybe since last Friday.

"Good. Because that's what I want from you, too. I love you, Tim. I think I always have—"

His lips descended and he kissed her. And even though it was a mostly chaste kiss, it still managed to make her panties damp. She heard nothing over the sound of her beating heart and Tim's rough breathing as he pulled away.

She realized they'd stopped swaying to the music she could barely even hear anymore, realized a few people were staring at them. She didn't care. Smiling up at him, she moved even closer.

"I love you, Gabby." His smile mirrored hers. "Now, either we dance. Or we leave. And since we just got here, and you look fucking amazing in that dress..."

They danced but they never made it to dinner.

THEY MADE it back to her place. Barely.

Tim had been undressing Gabby with his eyes since the moment she'd walked into the ballroom, but he'd tried to keep his desire under a tight hold while they were in public. He didn't want to embarrass her or himself by, oh, running his hand over her ass or adjusting a hard-on all night.

But now, finally, they were alone. She'd just closed and locked the door to her apartment behind them and had turned back to him, walking straight into his arms and lifting her mouth to his.

He let her kiss him, felt her hands cup his jaw as his hands wrapped around her waist to draw her into his body. For several minutes, all they did was kiss. Her lips moved over his, her tongue tangled with his, as her hands roamed his shoulders and chest.

He kept his hands locked to her hips, her midnight-blue dress slick and warm against his skin. His fingers curled into the material but released it just as quickly, afraid he'd rip it if he wasn't careful.

But when she rolled rubbed herself against his erection, he groaned and clamped his hands tighter on her hips.

Pulling away, he let his forehead rest against hers. "You're going to need to lose the dress."

She huffed out a laugh, her lips curving in a sexy little smile. "The big, tough hockey player can't deal with a little silk, huh?"

"This hockey player doesn't want to tear it off your hot body."

She hitched in a breath, her hands sliding to the back of his neck to run her nails up and down his nape.

"Maybe I want you to." Her smile turned wicked.

Heat raced through his body. "Gabby."

His voice held a distinct growl as he took a step back. She raised her eyebrows at him in challenge. Lust fired at her dare, the look she gave him pure provocation. If she wanted to play, he wasn't about to say no.

Grabbing her shoulders, he turned her until she had her back to him. Barely holding on to his control, he reached for the exposed zipper running down the back of the dress. Tugging it down, he watched it spill onto the ground. Then his gaze ran back up her body, taking in the peach lace panties that barely covered her ass and the bare expanse of her back. She hadn't been wearing a bra.

He swallowed hard, the tips of his fingers trailing up her spine from her waist to her neck, now uncovered by her hair, twisted in some kind of complicated knot, held together only by a couple of pretty sticks. When he pulled them out, her hair spilled down her back, making his cock jerk at the sight.

He left the panties. And the shoes. Holy hell, those shoes would be the death of him.

She looked over her shoulder at him, her gaze an invitation. Which he took.

Spinning her around, he kissed her again, his hands rising to cup her breasts, knead them, while her tongue slid along his. He felt her fingers working between them, his jacket being pushed off his shoulders until he had to release her so she could take it off.

His jacket and shirt disappeared in seconds, her nimble fingers falling to his pants. When she tugged the button through its hole, his cock responded by hardening even more. And when she shoved his pants down his legs, he put one hand on her nape and held her to him so he could kiss her even deeper.

But Gabby had other plans.

She went to her knees, her hands tugging down his boxer briefs. When his cock sprang free, he breathed a sigh of relief before drawing her head toward him. She gave some resistance but from the look she flashed him, he knew it was token, designed to make him even hotter. Which she was doing a damn fine job of.

The second her lips touched his cock, he wanted more. More of her mouth, more of her hands, her body. Wanted everything she had to give. And then some. He let her nuzzle him for a moment, rub the tip of her nose against the shaft, before she wrapped her hand around him and drew him into her mouth.

Damp heat. Tight suction. He'd be lucky not to hold off coming in seconds. He let her control the action, held himself steady as she sucked him with a rhythm that made him gasp.

Fuck. She made him crazy. Made him so fucking happy she was his.

As her hands gripped his thighs, kneading the tight muscles, his cock pulsed as her lips spread around the tip. With her eyes closed, she looked as if she were enjoying it almost as much as he was.

With reluctance, he pulled away from her mouth, sliding his hands under her arms to lift her. She wrapped her arms around his shoulders and her legs around his waist, his cock bumping against her mound, satin panties damp against his heated flesh.

Fuck yeah.

Keeping one arm around her back, he moved to the couch and lowered himself to the cushions. With his arm around her waist, he urged her higher, then used his free hand to guide his cock. He rubbed the tip against her panties, against her clit.

Her head fell back as her eyes closed, her bottom lip sucked between her teeth. Lowering his mouth to hers, he sealed their lips together for a deep kiss. As she moaned into his mouth, she angled her body so the head of his cock lodged between her lower lips, pushing her panties inside her body.

"Tim."

He knew what she wanted, wanted it just as much as she did. Pushing a hand between them, he tugged her panties to the side. The first touch of his cock against her pussy made them shudder, his arm around her waist tightening even more.

Somehow she managed to move, working herself against him until she slid onto his shaft. Aw, Christ, she might just kill him.

Groaning, he released her hips so she slid down until she couldn't go any farther.

"Gabby."

"Oh my god, you feel so good."

That was all it took to lose his control. He lifted her just high enough so that he felt her slide down his shaft. Her grip on him was so damn tight, it felt like a vise. But he slid easily because she was so wet.

Faster.

Her head tucked into his neck, her breath hot as a brand. His hips jerked, sinking him deeper. When she shuddered, he knew she was close. Their rhythm became harder, rougher.

He came, the pleasure so intense, he swore he saw stars. Gabby convulsed around him, her arms nearly cutting off his air supply. But he held on to her just as tightly.

"I love you."

He barely heard her, but he knew exactly the right words to say back.

"Love you, too."

DON'T MISS RJ's story in Deadlines & Red Lines.

ABOUT THE AUTHOR

Stephanie Julian is a USA Today and New York Times best-selling author of contemporary and paranormal romance.

Stay in touch for all new releases and sales by signing up for her newsletter on her website at stephaniejulian.com.

Reserve My Nights

Expose My Desire

Keep My Secrets

Rock My Heart

LOVERS UNDERCOVER

Lovers & Lies

Sinners & Secrets

Beauty & Brains

Thieves & Thrills

FORGOTTEN GODDESSES

What A Goddess Wants

How to Worship A Goddess

When A Goddess Falls

Where A Goddess Belongs

DARKLY ENCHANTED

Spell Bound

Moon Bound